Murder in
E-flat Major

To Jean —
Sorry not to have seen
you This year!
Best wishes to you & Zilly
Ron

Murder in E-flat Major

A Thomas Martindale Mystery

Ron Lovell

Printed in the United States of America
Library of Congress Control Number: 2010900212
ISBN: 978-0-9767978-7-6

Cover and book designer: Liz Kingslien
Editor: Mardelle Kunz
Cover bridge photo taken by Jet Lowe, 1990, "Perspective view from southwest"
Other photos: Splats and drips, iStock © Nicholas Monu; Treble Clef,
iStock © José Luis Gutiérrez
Back cover photo: Linda Hosek

Penman
PRODUCTIONS

P.O. Box 400, Gleneden Beach, Oregon 97388
www.martindalemysteries.com

SPECIAL THANKS TO:

*Stevie McDougal, whose knowledge of cellos
and symphony orchestras was invaluable.*

*Michele Longo Eder, whose "big case"
gave me the idea for the book.*

*Bob Webster, a friend since 1942,
whose financial support made this book possible.*

"*The man that hath no music in himself,*
Nor is not mov'd with concord of sweet sounds,
Is fit for treasons, stratagems, and spoils;
The motions of his spirit are dull as night,
And his affections dark as Erebus:
Let no such man be trusted."

— William Shakespeare, *The Merchant of Venice*

AS WE CLIMBED THE CIRCULAR IRON STAIRS *of the lighthouse, nudged along by the barrel of Maldanado's gun, I began to doubt that Maxine and I would make it out of here alive. The horrific noise of the storm would mask the sound of gunfire or our screams. As always, the drug dealer had the upper hand. He had ruined both of our lives very easily, with help from the idiotic local sheriff, Art Kutler. Maybe that grinning oaf, happy to add his own shove here and there on our upward passage, was smarter than I ever gave him credit for. His tips to the Mexican had enabled him to know where we were and how he could find us.*

As we ascended, the beam of Maldanado's flashlight illuminated the walls of the tower, which were bright and shining from a new coat of paint. The lighthouse renovation was almost complete after over a year of work in often difficult weather conditions. The Yaquina Head Lighthouse was about a mile from Highway 101 on a headland that has no protection from the often vicious storms that pound the Oregon coast each winter.

I loved this lighthouse and wished I was climbing the stairs as the unofficial tour guide I often served as for visiting friends and relatives. The thought crossed my mind that this might be my last climb. At least I would die with the woman I loved—Maxine March—whose arm I grabbed as we reached the lamp room at the top. Normally, small groups of people stood in this tight space while a guide told them all about the Fresnel lens that had magnified the light, which had shown from this tower since 1873. Then they would get to go up a small ladder far enough to poke their heads up to glance at the lens and view the breathtaking panorama of the rugged Oregon coast to the north and south.

Where was Paul Bickford? My good friend and protector had been with me below until he fell and Maldanado hit him on the head. That would stop most men, but Bickford was an officer in the Special Ops, an army unit trained to do the impossible. I guess I was expecting too much to think that he could survive such a blow. That memory made me dismiss any thoughts that he might rescue us. We were truly on our own.

As soon as the four of us were standing in the lamp room, Kutler pushed us through a door that was never opened to the public and out onto the wooden platform that had been built around the dome of the lighthouse to allow workmen to replace the windows and paint and sand-blast the rust-encrusted iron of the parapet and lantern housing. The lens had been covered to protect it from damage, and plastic sheathing had been draped over the top part of the lighthouse to shield the men from the incessant wind. We were standing in this temporary circular room that surrounded the dome; after the project was complete, this "room" would be torn down.

Maldanado used a knife to cut a hole in the plastic, allowing us to see both the upper part of the lighthouse and the surrounding area as no one had seen it before or would ever see again. The view of the waves hitting the rocks with a force that sent spray this high—over one hundred feet up—took my breath away. Despite my fear, I gloried in what I was seeing.

Maxine was not as sanguine. She was sobbing so hard that her body shook violently. I steadied her as best I could to keep her from collapsing as Maldanado pushed us back toward the side of the tower. The hapless sheriff stood off to one side with his gun still aimed at both of us.

Although the roar of the wind and the surf were very loud, I could hear the drug dealer as he spoke. "I want you to know that I never had anything against you, señorita," *he said to Maxine. "You were married to my brother so we are family. But now you know too much about my operation. Sadly, I have concluded that I cannot let you live."*

Then he turned to me. "As for you, my friend, you killed my brother—or caused him to be killed by your stupid meddling. Why did you stick your fuckin' nose where it did not belong?"

Just then I saw a slight movement in the doorway to Kutler's left. To distract their attention, I started talking about anything that came to mind. "What can I say? I've always been too curious for my own good. My editors and students always say that about me."

"Silencio!"

The drug dealer held up his gun to cut me off, but I kept talking. "Tell me this, Mr. Maldanado. How long has the sheriff been a part of your operation? I've never liked him, but I thought he was honest."

"You shut your trap!" growled Kutler, as he stiffened his arm and pointed his gun directly at me. "That's somethin' you're going to your grave wonderin' about. I know one thing: in a few minutes, you won't be causin' me any more troub . . ."

At that moment, Paul Bickford rushed out from the shadows under the iron girding of the lighthouse with such force that Kutler went flying through the air and out the opening to the sea, his cries lost in the relentless wind as he fell to his death.

Maldanado pushed me away and grabbed Maxine, holding a knife against her throat.

"I guess you've never faced someone who is as good a shot as I am," said Bickford, a smile on his face. "I guess you've never faced a killer who has had better training than you. You see, I'm a professional, honed into a killing machine by the United States Army. You learned only how to be a punk, and you rose to the top by killing other punks. You don't stand a chance, amigo."

And then Bickford pulled the trigger. Maxine screamed, and Maldanado looked surprised and touched his neck. Then he fell down and tried to get up.

By this time, blood was spurting from his neck. Bickford walked over to him and shot him again, this time in the head. Then he pushed him through the opening to the rocks and the ocean.

"You didn't see that," he said, throwing his gun out the same opening, as far and as high as he could.

Then he walked over to Maxine. "Are you okay, Maxie?"

He helped her to her feet, and she threw her arms around him and began to kiss him passionately on the lips and neck. I blinked in disbelief. Maxine and this good friend of mine—together? He was even calling her by the pet name I used. How had this happened? They barely knew each other. I backed away from this scene of betrayal.

"Now you know how it feels to be dumped on, Tom," she shouted. "Now you know how it feels to be taken for granted."

"I don't get it," I said. "I've always idolized you and tried to help you. I ruined my career for you."

Both she and Bickford laughed. As I stood there shaking my head, they kissed each other again and looked as though they could barely wait to tear off their clothes and go at it right here, howling winds and all.

"I'm sorry, Tom. . . . We are sorry," said Bickford, as he caught his breath after an especially passionate kiss. "There's no other way."

Both of them turned toward me and pushed. As I went out the opening of the shroud, I wondered if I would die of fright on the way down or be killed by the force of my body hitting the rocks.

✳ ✳ ✳ ✳ ✳

I had had this dream for several weeks. Each time, I woke up in a cold sweat, sitting upright in bed, my heart racing. I was glad no one else was in the house and that neighbors did not live nearby, because I was certain I had screamed.

WINTER 2006

WINTER ON THE OREGON COAST TESTS THE METTLE of those who live here all the time. We are not people who love the area for mild temperatures and endless sunny days. We are not people who expect quiet seas and no wind. If we wanted that kind of weather, we would live in California—and be bored and get sick of all that perfection. Living on the Oregon coast year-round is not for sissies.

I thought of this as I lay in my bed listening to the steady beating of rain on the roof and the occasional gust of wind that rattled the windows. The violent storm matched my dark mood. I was depressed—not in the clinical sense where I needed to see a psychiatrist, but just sad most days.

My bad dreams didn't help. They brought back memories I wanted to forget—of danger and loss and regret. Every night for two weeks I had had the same nightmare, and I was sick of it. It had so disturbed me that I tended to dwell on it daily, allowing my negative thoughts to push everything else out of my mind. Along with the bad dreams, I had night sweats and was losing weight. In the back of my mind, I feared that I was suffering from some kind of PTSD—posttraumatic stress disorder—the ailment that military people get after too much time in combat. Maybe that was stretching things a bit, but I knew my attitude was becoming a real problem.

Since my brief arrest for murder and subsequent quick release from jail, my career as a journalism professor at Oregon University had been on hold. My position was never in danger once I was cleared of all charges, but the whole incident had made me paranoid. The normal gossipy nature of a university community can be interesting and even fun, as long as you aren't the subject of all the nasty talk. Since my life had unraveled, I found myself the target of innuendo and rumor, which made it unbearable for me to be on campus, at least in the short term. At this point, I didn't want to go back. The university had granted me a one-year leave without pay, which meant that my position would be waiting for me when, and if, I returned.

Luckily for me, a way out had appeared, almost by magic, at my darkest hour. A literary agent had contacted me to write a book about my experiences with the drug gang, including my time in hiding in the Arctic and eventual return to Oregon for the so-called "showdown" that kept giving me the disturbing dreams.

Because the details had been so fresh in my mind, I wrote the book in six months. I have always been a fast writer, a trait I picked up during my years in magazine journalism where you'd face the wrath of your editor if you missed a deadline because your precious prose was not ready to face the reading public. I always told my students that if a film were ever to be made of me in the process of writing, it would not show a corner of my study filling up with crumpled pieces of paper as I agonized over every word and sentence. I usually blasted through the whole work as fast as I could and then took my pleasure in the revision process.

After news of my adventure became public, I was contacted by the agent, who worked in Los Angeles. She urged me to prepare an outline and several chapters of what had happened to me. Although I had written hundreds of articles and several textbooks in my career, I had never considered doing a book for the general public. Mainstream fiction and nonfiction was a different world from the journalistic and academic one I was used to. But the idea intrigued me, and I finished the submission in a week.

A few days later, the agent called and offered to represent me. She even flew up to Oregon to meet me and have me sign the agreement. I liked Janet Scott the minute I met her at the Portland airport. She was funny and smart. We had lunch nearby because she was on her way to New York for meetings with publishers. She planned to show my outline and chapters to publishers there. "I can't promise anything," she said, "but I'd love to get one of these houses to offer you a contract."

A week later, she called with the news that a small publisher in New York wanted to bring the book out as soon as I could finish writing it. I signed the contract when she faxed it to me and got to work, marveling at the speed in which this was all taking place. If things went like I hoped they would, I could leave the university and start making my living as a writer of books. No more whispers, no more pitying looks from colleagues, no more boring meetings. I would only miss the students.

I finished writing the book in five months and took another month to edit it. I worked with an editor at the publishing house—Flatiron Press, named for the historic building where its offices were located in New York City—and was soon reading galley proofs.

I reached over and picked up the advance copy of *The Cocaine Trail* from my bedside table and held it in both hands. I sat up and leafed through the pages. That is one of the thrills of writing a book—to be able to hold it and know that you had done what only a few people ever do. Talk is cheap when it comes to writing. Many people plan to do a book and may write a few hundred words, but few have the discipline or the time to see it through. "Writing is easy," wrote the late, great sportswriter Red Smith. "You sit in front of a typewriter until beads of blood form on your forehead."

The trill of my cell phone broke my reverie. I got up and walked into the living room where I had left it on a table. I shivered a bit at the coldness of the room as I pressed the "talk" button.

"Hello."

"Good morning, Tom. Janet Scott here. Are you decent?"

"Depends on your definition of that word," I said.

"Let's not go there this early in the morning," she said with a laugh. "Sorry to call so early, but I need to talk to you about some book signings I've arranged. They won't start until spring, except I think I'll set up one in Portland soon so you can get your feet wet."

"Great. I'm really happy to be doing something I've dreamed about for years."

"Be careful what you wish for, Tom. Going on the book trail is not as glamorous as it sounds. It's hard work, and you'll have to suffer a few fools along the way."

"Given some of the colleagues I work with in my department, I've got lots of experience with that kind of thing."

"Yeah, same for me in my business," she said. "Would that the world of work was full of smart people like you and me—or is it 'you and I'?"

When you teach writing, people always think you are lying in wait to correct their grammar.

"Beats the hell out of me," I replied.

"Do you have any preferences for where you want to go?"

"No, I'll leave it up to you, Janet. Just send me to places where people will buy hundreds of my books."

"Now *that* is truly the general idea," she laughed. "I'm glad you are such a fast learner. Okay, I'll make some calls and set up some dates for you. You know the publisher will not be paying for any of this travel. It's a small company, and they just don't have the budget."

"No grand tour with first-class plane tickets and rooms at five-star hotels? I am appalled."

"Welcome to the real world of publishing," she continued. "The companies spend the money to tour people who don't need to tour—I mean like politicians and movie stars. Their books will sell anyway."

"I'm kidding. I know all of this, and I don't care. I applied for and got some travel money from the university. It should cover some travel with maybe one jaunt to the East, if you can book me back there."

"That's good news. I will do that and call you tomorrow. I want to get going on this and get you out there as soon as the book is officially released."

We finished our call and I took a shower, happy in the knowledge that my life might just have turned a corner.

AFTER BREAKFAST, I STRAIGHTENED UP THE HOUSE and then drove up Highway 101 to the Wildflower Grill in Lincoln City, the next large town up the coast from Newport. I was meeting Michaela Ross for lunch. I had met "Mike"—as she preferred to be called—at a cocktail party the previous Christmas at the home of a mutual friend, the director of a local theater group. We hit it off immediately and when I told her that I needed an interesting volunteer activity, she invited me to join the board of the Oregon Coast Symphony Orchestra.

The owner of the Wildflower gave me a big hug as I walked in the door. Vickie probably did that to everyone, but it made me feel special.

"You're getting too thin," she said, as she stepped back to eye me up and down. "You need to come here more often and eat."

"That's the pot calling the kettle black," I laughed. Vickie was as thin as a model.

"Are you calling me an old pot?" she asked, as she winked, picked up a menu, and led me out into the large room in the back that overlooked a pretty wetland area.

"I'll need another menu. I'm meeting someone."

"Stepping out on me again," she said and winked again.

We walked to a table in the corner, and I sat down.

"Tony will be right here to get your beverage order. I'll drop by later to see who my competition is."

I glanced at the menu, although I knew it by heart.

"Someone is joining you, Tom?"

"Hi, Tony. Yes."

Tony was a pleasant young man and a good waiter. I always kidded him about the theatrical flourish with which he did his job. He placed food in front of customers as though it was a work of art. He even poured the water by raising the pitcher high in the air so the contents would kind of cascade down into the glass.

"Did I read that you were involved in some kind of incident?" Tony asked.

"Yeah, I guess that is a good way to describe it," I replied. "I'd call it more like a period of unpleasantness."

Tony jotted down a few words on the back of his order pad—he wanted to be a writer. "I've not heard that phrasing before."

"When are you going to go back to college?" I asked. I like to give people advice about how to run their lives. "You'll never be a writer if you don't get some formal training."

He glanced around conspiratorially before responding. "I know, I know, but I don't want to leave Vick in the proverbial lurch. Is that the proper use of 'proverbial'?"

"Yeah, it is. I see your point and I don't blame you, but she wouldn't want to hold you back."

"I'll do it eventually, but I've got to keep saving money."

"At least start keeping a journal."

"What would I put in it? My life's kinda dull."

"Write about the people you meet here. Good ones, bad ones. Of course, the latter make for the best stories."

"Here is your guest, Tom."

I stood up to greet Mike as Vickie led her to the table.

"Michaela Ross, this is the owner of this fine establishment, Vickie Drake, and her faithful sidekick, Tony Valentino."

Mike shook hands all around, then the other two walked away.

I pulled out a chair and she sat down, placing a large purse on the floor beside her. She reached in and pulled out a pair of glasses.

"Vanity, vanity. I should wear them all the time."

"I went through that stage myself, but now I just put them on and think they make me look professorial."

"They do indeed," she smiled.

Mike looked to be in her fifties. She was dressed casually but still had a regal air about her. Maybe I was reacting to her career as a concert cellist. Had she performed for thirty years in a rock band, I would probably not have had the same impression.

"Something to drink?" Tony had returned.

"Hot tea with lemon for me," Mike said.

"Iced tea," I said.

He wrote down our drink orders. "Have we decided on our food?"

"The crab salad with house dressing on the side," she said.

"Good choice," he said.

"Half a ham sandwich with Swiss and soup for me. What is the soup?"

"Cream of asparagus."

"The soup is always good here, Mike. Want to try a cup?"

"Okay. You twisted my arm."

Tony departed.

"It's good to see you again," I said. "I appreciate your suggestion about joining the symphony board. I've been on maybe a hundred committees at the university but never a community one involving volunteers."

"Just like the people you probably dealt with on your campus committees, I'm afraid we have our share of foolish people," she laughed, as she sipped her tea, "although maybe the ones here are not as well educated."

"So, what would I have to do?"

"Here we are, folks," said Tony, as he placed the food-laden plates in front of us.

Mike blinked.

"You always get your money's worth at Wildflower. Lots of food."

"Ground pepper on your salad?"

Tony stood poised with a large pepper mill held high was if it were a weapon.

Mike shook her head and I did too.

"Enjoy your lunches."

"As a board member, we would ask you to attend monthly meetings and to do some other tasks," she said, between bites of salad. "With your background, you'd be ideal for marketing and public relations."

"I'm not sure. Would I have to do any fundraising? I hate to ask people for money."

"No, we have a person on the board who specializes in writing grant proposals and lining up big donors. We've got a pretty healthy endowment for an organization of this small size."

"Let me think about it. What is your role on the board, Mike?"

"I'm the liaison to the orchestra but also a full voting member. I bring the concerns of the musicians to the attention of the board and vice versa, board to musicians. Before I came along, the music director was the one who conveyed our opinions and requests to the board. We decided we did not want that filter."

"You said you played in the Oregon Symphony before moving here?"

"For thirty years."

"You must have started there as a teenager."

"Thanks, I think. I was awfully young when I had the good luck to audition there and get hired. It just kind of clicked for me, and I loved it."

"Why the cello?"

"Do you want the long answer or the short one?"

"Long one, please. I don't have anywhere to go."

Old friends accuse me of interviewing people even in casual conversation. People like to talk about themselves, and what they say is usually interesting. Besides, it keeps me from having to talk about myself.

"Okay, here goes, but stop me if you get bored. My mother was born in Lebanon, and she and my father met when he was studying at the American University in Beirut. When he finished his year there, they got married and returned to Walla Walla, Washington, where he had grown up. After law school at the University of Washington, he opened a law practice in that town. I came along a year later.

"I am an only child and grew up in a home where every wish was my command. Added to that was the fact that my parents loved music. We used to listen to opera on the radio every Saturday morning, for example. Walla Walla has the oldest continuously operating symphony in the West, so the town had a long musical heritage. My parents wanted me to have music lessons—the violin—and my teacher was a player in that orchestra. I remember that the trunk of his car was filled with violins. I picked one out and learned to play it. I was in something called 'The Junior String' when I was a fifth grader. Sometime in there, my mother took me to Seattle to see the film *Night at Carnegie Hall*. It was a performance by an orchestra with a cellist who carried his cello like a spear. That memory stuck with me, and in the seventh grade, I switched to the cello. I got better and better, and when I was in the ninth grade, I was invited to become a member of the Walla Walla Symphony."

"Pretty young," I said. "You were a child prodigy."

She blushed. "Well, I don't know about that, but I was pretty good at an early age. I went on to a small liberal arts college in the Midwest and majored in music. Of course, I continued with the cello. After I graduated, I went to the School of Music at Indiana University for a master's degree. At some point near the end of that program, various orchestras held auditions at the school, and I went to the one put on by the Oregon Symphony. And I was hired."

I shook my head. "A truly meteoric rise."

"At that time, the symphony was still in the minor leagues. The season lasted from October 1 to March 1. Players were only paid for the days they worked—$19 for rehearsals, $25 for performances. I worked part-time as the secretary to a psychologist."

"Have we saved room for dessert?" Tony had returned to pick up our plates and refill our drinks.

"The marionberry cobbler is really good here," I said.

"Will you split it with me?" Mike asked.

I nodded.

"I'll bring two forks," said Tony.

"So, here you are, this kid from a smallish town with this big instrument you excelled at playing about to fulfill your dream. It seems to me that you'd get a lot of satisfaction from playing this wonderful music and bringing it to the world."

"I think people love classical music, and I guess music in general, because it has a beat, like a heartbeat. Even as a listener, you feel it."

"I'm afraid that I can't get into modern classical music," I said. "All that dissonance and off-kilter sound. For me, a lot of it is like listening to chalk on a blackboard."

"Someone in music, I'm not sure who, said that every piece of music has the right to be played once," she added. "In some cases, it's so dreadful that it needs to be put back on the shelf—maybe forever. But that is not true for the classic pieces we all know and love. I guess my love affair with the music and the playing of it will be with me forever.

"But, there is a downside, like there is with everything in life," she continued. "Being in the orchestra for so long has damaged my hearing because of being seated in front of the trumpet section for thirty years. You can't wear earplugs because you need to hear yourself play. Some orchestras have plastic shields in front of the horns, and that helps. Another problem is the way you have to sit to play a cello—on the edge of your chair. You need a flat-bottom chair to be comfortable."

"But, in spite of all of this, you love to play your cello in a symphony orchestra," I said.

"You noticed that I get all dewy-eyed when I talk about it," she said, before laughing. "You are right, I do love it."

"You never really said why you switched from violin to cello those many years ago. For one thing, it's big and bulky."

"Yes, I guess I didn't. I love the sound. It is the closest to a human voice of any musical instrument. It has an enormous range, from the midrange of a piano to as high as a violin. At the same time, it can be mellow."

"Is your cello real old?"

"It's over two hundred years old. It was made by Thomas Dodd in 1780. My parents bought it for me for about $2,000. Now, it is priceless. It seems to get better with age."

"Would that we could all make that statement."

Michaela threw back her head and chortled. "Boy, you got that right." She looked at her watch. "I'm due to give a music lesson in a half-hour. I'd better get going." She reached for the check.

"My treat," I said. "I appreciate the information. I always like to know the people I'm working with and also a bit about new subjects.

Journalists and professors carry around a lot of disconnected information in their heads, but this was something new to me."

"I'll get it next time. You know, I got so carried away with telling you about myself, we didn't talk about you. I guess you're used to asking the questions. Also, we didn't get into much about the board."

"You know, on second thought, I don't think I'll be joining the board," I said. "I would probably wind up resenting the time I put in. I seem to have this passion to be creative. For me, that means writing every day. While we were sitting here, I was thinking that I would like to write a profile of you."

"Really? I'm flattered, but I'm not sure how interested anybody else would be to read what you write." She thought for a moment and then said, "Sure, why not?"

"Great. I'd also like to get a behind-the-scenes look at how the orchestra operates."

"I think I can arrange that," she said. "I'll get back to you."

We gathered our things and walked to the front where I left the money on the counter. After waving to Vickie and Tony, who were busy with other customers, we walked out the door and ran to our cars through the drenching deluge.

A WEEK LATER, I DROVE TO PORTLAND for my trial run appearance in a bookstore with my new book. I guess calling it an "appearance" makes it sound a bit theatrical, like I was some kind of movie or TV star. I was far from that, wanting only to sell as many books as I could and talk to readers and potential readers.

This was new to me. When you write textbooks or academic treatises, no one ever wants you to autograph their copies. Indeed, students probably hate the authors whose words their instructors assign them to read. Selling textbooks is a lot different too. Instructors decide what to use, then bookstores place their orders. The books sell twenty and thirty at a time.

With trade books, the opposite occurs. People buy one book at a time, and it is up to you, as an author talking to people about your book at signings or other events—and the publisher, by making the book attractive with a good cover and good design and a reasonable selling price—to make the sale. It was almost like hand-to-hand combat, author versus potential reader.

My agent and I had chosen to launch my book in a bookstore specializing in mysteries and true crime books. I might go later to some big chain stores, but I wanted my debut to be more personal. I had met the owner of the store, Hannah Graves—no pun intended—at an event for another author at her store the year before. I told her about my project, and she asked me to consider doing a signing when the book came out. I told my agent to set it up and here I was, entering the store at 6:30 p.m. on a Friday night in February. Mercifully, the weather had improved to the extent that I could get over the Coast Range without worrying about driving home on snowy or icy roads. Sometimes February was like that, with maybe a two-week lull between the rains and winds of January and the bluster of March.

"Hello, Hannah."

She looked up from a table halfway back in the narrow room where she was arranging cheese, crackers, and cookies on plates. I noticed a dish of peanuts too. Bottles of sparkling cider and a coffee urn sat on the rear of the table.

"Tom, welcome. So good to see you. Thanks for launching your book with us."

I hugged her.

"My pleasure. Thank you for having me here. This is my debut on the signing circuit so you'll have to forgive me if I foul up. It's all new to me."

She returned to the table.

"So I stand over there?" I motioned to a smaller table around which folding chairs had been arranged. The store was divided into sections by bookshelves that jutted out here and there down the length of the store.

"Oh, yes, sorry. I tend to fuss over this food too much." She walked back to the other table. "You can stand here behind this table with your books. There is a box of them over there on the floor, and I've made a display in the window and at the front counter. I'll introduce you, and then you can give your talk. After that, we might have some questions from the audience. People like to talk to real live authors."

She smiled, but I had the thought that I might feel like a monkey in the zoo under such scrutiny.

"What should I say?"

"Different authors do different things. Talk about writing the book. Read an excerpt. Some people may ask about how to get their own work published."

"It sounds pretty easy. I should be able to talk about the how and why. After all, it's my book. I should be the expert."

It would be easy, and I did not feel nervous, only a bit uncertain since this was my first time. And I figured the audience would be much more appreciative than a classroom full of bored undergraduates.

Hannah walked to the front of the store, so I walked to the table and sat down in the chair behind it. I opened my advance copy in which I had placed some Post-its in various places throughout the book. I imagined that the trick in reading excerpts was to pick places that would arouse interest but could also stand on their own for an audience that had not read the book.

In a few minutes, the front door opened and five people walked in. After stopping at the front counter, they moved toward the back of the store, two pausing to eat cheese and crackers and pour cider, while the other three sat down.

"Are you the author?" asked an older woman in a coat that was several sizes too big for her. She was wearing a beret and a long scarf, which she proceeded to unwind very deliberately.

"Yes, I am. Thank you for coming."

She continued to work on the scarf and turned her back on me, now that she had established who I was.

"How are you two?" I asked the other two people who were apparently a couple. "Nice to have a break in the bad weather."

The woman looked frightened that I had spoken to her and looked down. "I prefer the snow and cold," said the man. "I get my exercise shoveling snow."

"Oh yeah, sure," I said lamely.

"Around here, all you get to do is shovel rain," said the scarf lady. She apparently liked her little joke because she began to laugh, quietly at first, then so forcefully that it overwhelmed her air passage and she started to cough.

I stood up.

Hannah rushed from the front with a cup of water. "Are you all right, Gertrude?"

"I'm fine," she croaked between wheezy gasps and waved us both away.

The first three were soon joined by five older ladies who seemed to be together. One of them, a small lady with blue hair and a friendly face, stepped forward.

"Mr. Tom Martindale—or is it Professor Thomas Martindale?"

"Tom is fine, ma'am."

She turned to the others. "He said we could call him Tom." She turned back to me. "That is thrilling. We are part of a book group, The Deadly Readers, and we buy all of our books here. And we love to meet authors in the flesh."

"I've got plenty of that," I laughed, as I extended my hand.

"He's says he's got plenty of flesh," she said, again turning to her fellow group members, "but he looks pretty skinny to me."

Turning back to me, she scrutinized me up and down. "You could use some meat on those bones."

I blushed.

Again, to the others: "He's blushing."

"I've been kind of under the weather for a while."

"Not enough damn snow," grumbled the man with the mousy wife.

"Whatever," said the book group leader. "I want to thank you for sharing your talent with us, professor . . . I mean Tom. We appreciate that."

"I guess you won't really know about the talent part until you read my book."

"By the way, will this be available in the library?"

"I'm not sure about that. Of course, I'm here to sell my books."

"He says he's here to sell books," she said to the others.

It was nice to have an interpreter. I smiled faintly. One of the two worst things an author hears is that a would-be reader is planning to get his book in the library. Then the woman mentioned the other one.

"Well, we'll at least buy one copy and pass it around!"

Hannah cleared her throat as five more people took their places in the folding chairs.

"I guess that's the signal for me to sit down and shut up," said the woman. "By the way, I'm Muriel Campbell. I've got a great idea for a book, and I want you to help me with it. We'll talk later."

"Well . . . er . . . sure."

"Our guest tonight is Tom Martindale," began Hannah. "As most of you know, this store specializes in fiction, mystery fiction. But we have always carried a number of books that are classified in the book trade as true crime. Tom Martindale's new book, *The Cocaine Trail*, is such a book. Tom not only wrote the book, he also lived through many of the events he describes in the book. Please welcome Tom Martindale."

I stood up to a smattering of applause and picked up my copy of the book.

"Good evening and thank . . ."

"Could you speak a little louder?" shouted the scarf lady.

I ignored her but did try to raise the decibel level of my voice to just below a shout.

"As Hannah mentioned, my new book, *The Cocaine Trail*, is partly a story I lived through. Several years ago, I became aware of the activities of a colleague on the Oregon University faculty—a biologist—who was conducting unauthorized and illegal research into the deadly Ebola virus. You may have already heard about that virus in the news over the past twenty years. It breaks out in Africa from time to time, and those who get it die fairly quickly of massive hemorrhaging. There is no cure or even treatment. It is probably transmitted by monkeys. The virus usually rages for a few weeks, a lot of people die, and then it retreats back into the jungle to lie in wait."

"Like a lunatic," said the scarf lady with a shudder.

"Shhhhhhhh!" said Muriel Campbell, glaring at the scarf lady.

"At any rate, the research efforts on finding a cure or a successful treatment for Ebola have been few and far between. Anyone who succeeded in doing either or both of these feats would be famous overnight. Their career would be enhanced. This colleague I mentioned—the biologist—decided to work on the virus full-time. His efforts at first seemed promising but there was one catch: he planned to use human subjects, not the normal monkeys or rats and mice. And the subjects were Mexican migrants whom he transported into this country illegally. They did not, of course, know what they were getting involved in. Women, children, and old men were all brought into the United States under false pretenses, unaware that they were to be subjected to research protocols that would rival the Nazis—research protocols that would most certainly kill them."

There were gasps from the audience. The scarf lady looked as if she might faint. Muriel Campbell started to cry. Even the gruff snow shovel man seemed moved.

"That dirty bastard!" he yelled rising to his feet, as his mousy wife tried to restrain him.

"I know it is tough to hear all of this, but it is true," I continued, hoping to calm them down. I had to admit that their reactions held the promise of good sales for the book. Crass and commercial as that seemed, I needed high sales if I was ever to get to the point of supporting myself as a full-time writer of books.

"This is where I came in. When I discovered what this guy was trying to do, I brought it to the attention of the proper authorities and he was eventually caught."

"Good for you, Professor Tom," said Muriel Campbell, the others in her book group nodding in agreement and smiling at me.

"As all good stories have a tendency to do, this one had many twists and turns. Like the fact that this biologist had a half brother who was the leader of a drug gang and was smuggling large quantities of cocaine into Oregon."

"Those dirty bastards," yelled the snow shovel man again, his wife looking as if she wanted to melt into the floor at his outburst.

"In doing what I did to bring down the biologist, however, I made an enemy of the drug guy. As a result, I had to go into hiding for a while."

"You went undercover?" asked the scarf lady.

"Not exactly."

"Witness intervention?" asked Muriel Campbell, her book group cohorts eager for my answer.

"It's called Witness Protection, madam," corrected the snow shovel man.

"Not anything as formal as that," I continued. "But I did leave the continental United States. I went to the Arctic as part of a media tour with the Coast Guard while its scientists studied global warming. That got me away from here and gave me some measure of safety. It's all in my book."

I stopped talking and sat down behind the table containing the books. I hadn't realized that talking about all of these rather traumatic events would take their toll on me. I was tired.

"I think I'll stop here and answer your questions."

As I gazed out at the people sitting in front of me, a familiar face smiled at me from the area near the refreshment table. Lorenzo Madrid had been my lawyer a few years ago. It was because of him that I was not now spending time in jail.

I smiled at him and mouthed the words "Stick around?"

He nodded.

"Well then, ladies and gentlemen, I'd be happy to answer your questions."

Naturally, the scarf lady was the first to speak.

"Do you compose your books on a computer, or do you write them in longhand?"

"Oh, for Pete's sake, what kind of a question is that?" thundered the snow shovel man. "He's got a serious subject here, and you want to talk about penmanship. Ridiculous!"

"At least I have a reason to ask about technique and procedures," she replied huffily. "From what I've seen of you here, I am sure you would not be capable of writing anything intelligent."

He leaped to his feet, his wife looking like she was on the verge of collapse. "That is a damn outrage. I won't . . ."

Good grief, they were worse than kindergarten students.

"I don't mind answering questions about the *way* I write, although I hope you'll also ask me about *what* I write," I smiled, hoping to defuse the feud.

The man sat down, and the woman turned back to face me. I was glad they were not sitting next to each other—they might have come to blows.

"I used to write all of my longer pieces out in longhand on yellow legal pads using pencils, a pile of perfectly sharpened ones on the desk. I thought the computer would be too mechanical and interfere with my creativity. Then I had to have a typist try to figure out my handwriting to do the next draft. Of course, I never did that with magazine pieces when I was a working journalist. When you write books that way—in pencil on a yellow pad—you add extra time to the process. Still, I did it that way for far too long. So when it came time to write *The Cocaine Trail*, I decided to compose on my computer. And you know what? It did not hamper my creative process, and it was a lot faster. What a concept! I finally joined the twentieth century, although by this time we were in the twenty-first."

They all smiled at that remark, even the warring duo.

"I would say, write in whatever way you feel comfortable with. The important thing is to write. Yes, ma'am? . . ."

The leader of the reading group had her hand up.

"Was it hard to write about things you had experienced yourself?"

"Good question. Yes, at times it was. I had always been trained as a journalist to keep myself out of the story. Unless you are an editorial writer or someone doing analysis pieces, you keep yourself and your opinions out of the story. In this case, of course, I was intimately involved in all aspects of the story. I could not remain on the sidelines and pretend otherwise. At the same time, I wanted to be as ethical and truthful as I could. I kept that goal in mind as I wrote the book and urged my editors to look for unfair bias as they read the manuscript."

A younger woman in the back who had not yet spoken raised her hand. She was wearing a long, black dress and had multiple piercings in both ears and alongside her nose, giving her a Goth look.

"Yes, ma'am? . . ."

"The woman you refer to as "M"—is she a real person or a composite?"

"She is a real person. I felt I had to protect her in the book because she was a key witness in the government's case against the drug dealers and was, for a time, in the Witness Protection program we talked about before. I thought it might be best to keep her profile low."

"Isn't it true that you were linked romantically with her in the past and stepped into her life after her husband was killed?"

There were looks of shock on the faces of the rest of the audience.

I was amused that these people were feeling protective of me.

"Shame on you, young lady!" said the scarf lady.

"You should be ashamed of yourself," added the snow shovel man.

"That's okay," I said. "If I published this book, I ought to be able to respond to questions about it. Who are you with?"

"Oh, wow. I didn't mean to cause such a stir," she said. "I'm Rachel, with the Under-the-Book-Cover dot com blog. We give our readers an inside look at the publishing world."

"I'm sure you do," I smiled. It would be easy to demolish her before this crowd of people who were rooting for me, but I might be sorry when the blog appeared later that night. Readers were readers, and I couldn't afford to alienate any of them. I decided instead to kill her with kindness.

"The woman in question is an old friend, and I met her during the course of my investigation of the biologist I talk about in the book. At that time, she was his *former* wife, and she became very much his victim. Our friendship had no bearing on the case against him. It's all detailed in the book. I don't know where you got this information, but it's not true, and I hope you'll check your facts next time. I'm always happy to help reporters with their stories. Heck, I was a reporter myself and, I hope, still am."

I smiled at the blog lady as other members of the audience murmured their approval. I heard more than one "he's such a nice young man" coming from The Deadly Readers delegation. I hoped she wouldn't disparage me too much online. People who write blogs or have their own Web sites can do damage to whomever they target—even if their facts are wrong—but there is little one can do to stop them. Veiled cooperation and hope for fairness was the best I could do at the moment.

"We have time for one more question," said Hannah, who joined me at the table. "Yes? . . ."

A short man in a big overcoat and Russian-style fur hat stood up.

"I vas vundering, if you please, to help me with my story of life in Warsaw in the Polish ghetto in 1939 ven I vas only child—I mean little kid."

"That sounds like a great story," I said, hoping to let him down easily. His was probably a dramatic story but, unfortunately, not all that unique in recent years as various anniversaries of World War II events occurred. "I would suggest you consider publishing your story yourself, for your family perhaps."

"I haf no family, sir. I am forever alone."

More murmurs from the crowd, this time of sympathy.

The scarf lady stood up and walked over to him. "I am in a writing group at my church, and we would love to have you join us. I write family history, and maybe I can give you some tips and work with you on this."

She patted his hand as tears rolled down his face.

"That seems like a wonderful idea," I said, hesitating to break the tender moment. "If you'd like to buy my book, I'd be happy to sign copies, at no extra charge."

They smiled, and Hannah hurriedly stacked the books on the table in front of me. I darted over to the refreshments table and poured a cup of apple cider and grabbed a cookie.

"Great to see you," I said to Lorenzo. "This will only take about fifteen minutes. Can I buy you dinner? There's a nice little Italian place right across the street."

"I'd like nothing better," he said. "I'll go over there and get us a table."

I returned to the books table and sat down, shoving a cookie in my mouth and taking a sip of cider.

"Thanks for your kind remarks," I said to the book group lady.

"I just love meeting a real author. Sign it 'To Gloria.' She's my granddaughter, and she wants to be a writer after she works as an astronaut."

"Well, that will be an interesting combination."

I quickly scribbled "To Gloria—Good luck in your career."

"Could you put 'Professor' in front of your name? I want to tell her that I met a real writer who is a real professor."

"Sure. Glad to do that."

A member of the book group was next in line.

"Just sign it. I may give it as a gift."

Or sell it on eBay, I thought to myself as I signed my name.

"Thanks for coming."

"That old gal's got a heart after all," said the snow shovel man, who was up next. "I was ready to ring her neck until she stepped up to help that old foreign guy. Just put 'To Nadine, never a mystery to me'." His mousy wife looked lovingly at him. "Oh, Elmer. How sweet."

They moved on.

"I already told you my name."

It was the scarf lady, exacting her revenge. She was daring me to remember her name. I have to admit that I am bad with names. It has always taken me half the term to learn the names of my students to the extent that I could greet them when I saw them out of the classroom. I never forgot a face but had never had the politician's skill at knowing who was who. I opened the book slowly as I racked my brain.

"Gertrude," said Hannah, who was suddenly standing next to me at the table. "I think you will love this book. You know, I've never steered you wrong in all the years you've been coming in here."

Saved, and not for the first time in my life.

"To Gertrude," I wrote. "Thanks for your kindness to a person in need. Best wishes, Tom Martindale."

LORENZO MADRID WAS SITTING AT A TABLE near the front window looking at a menu when I walked into the restaurant. He got up when I reached the table, and we embraced.

"What a pleasant surprise to see you at my signing. How long has it been—a year, year and a half?"

"Sounds about right," he said. "Right in the middle of that stuff with the nasty scientist and his wife—the woman you were accused of killing."

"And you got me off with an ease that still amazes me when I think of it."

He smiled. "It's not that hard to do when the evidence in a case is so skimpy."

"So, what brings you to Portland?"

"I've just finished attending a two-day legal seminar at the convention center. I saw the notice of your book signing in the paper this morning and decided to drop by to see you."

"I'm really glad you did."

Lorenzo studied the menu. "I gather you've been here before. What's good?"

"I come here whenever I'm at the bookstore since it's so close.

I've had the veal Parmesan and the lasagna and spaghetti and meat-balls. How about some wine?"

The waitress had arrived. I nodded at Lorenzo.

"Spaghetti and meatballs and some house red."

The young woman seemed transfixed by Lorenzo. He was a handsome man—his bronzed skin and dark hair setting off teeth so white that they blinded you when he smiled, which he did a lot. In his movie star good looks, he resembled the Spanish actor Antonio Banderas.

"I'd like to order too," I said, after a minute or two of delay as the waitress stared at Madrid.

"Oh, yeah, sorry," she mumbled. "What'll you have?"

"Lasagna, salad with Italian dressing, and a glass of red."

She wrote down my order but was still looking at Lorenzo.

"Miss."

No movement.

"Miss?"

"Oh, sorry. What?"

"Could we also have two glasses of water and some bread?"

She nodded and wandered off, no doubt lost in her thoughts of being swept up in Lorenzo's arms and carried onboard a galleon on the Spanish Main.

"Do you get that a lot?"

"Get what?"

"Women staring at you and undressing you with their eyes."

He blushed. "Oh, kind of, but I don't pay any attention to it. It's just chick stuff. I'm no stud, believe me. I work too much and too hard to spend much time on a social life, much less a sex life."

"That I find hard to believe. Anyway, tell me about yourself. How's your practice going? Still doing a lot of pro bono cases and are you still in Salem?"

"Yes and yes," he smiled, taking a sip of wine and a bite of bread.

"My people need me. I spend most of my time on immigration stuff—people being deported or taken advantage of by unscrupulous landlords and dishonest farmers. They hire whole families and make them live in rat-infested houses with leaky roofs and no indoor plumbing, then try to get out of paying them when their work is done. It is bad."

"Do you do any high-profile cases anymore, like I guess I was?"

"Yes, now and then. It keeps my coffers full and allows me to take the cases I really like, the ones where I help my people and see that they receive the justice they deserve."

"Had any interesting ones lately?"

"No, but I might be in line for a few. I've joined up with a consortium of lawyers around the country who are concentrating on people who have been wrongly accused under the Patriot Act."

"Let's see, the Patriot Act was the one passed right after the 9/11 terrorist attacks that suspends a lot of legal rights?"

"That it does," he said, as he started to eat his salad. "Under the Patriot Act, which was rammed through Congress by the Bush administration in the climate of fear just after 9/11, the government is allowed to circumvent the Fourth Amendment—the one that prevents unreasonable searches and seizures without probable cause—if a special court okays it. That has opened up a whole new can of worms, and we fear that people can be arrested on the slimmest of evidence if federal agents believe they have done something wrong. The Feds don't need as much evidence as they did in the past."

"Sounds like *1984* to me," I said. "Very scary. I know how trapped I felt, even for just the few hours until you got me out of jail. Have you been involved in any cases like this yet?"

"Not so far, but those of us participating in the project want to be ready. The Bushies have really created a climate of fear in this country. Innocent people could be arrested on trumped-up charges under the cover of national security. This is a new kind of war, no doubt, but in fighting it, we don't have to trample all over the Constitution."

Our food arrived. While setting down my plate, the waitress tipped over my water glass because she was looking at Lorenzo instead of looking where she put my plate.

"Careful!" I shouted, as I jumped up to prevent the water from running down my leg.

"Oh, gee, did I do that?" she said dreamily.

"Just get me a couple of napkins, and I'll mop up the water."

She seemed frozen in place but an older woman—the owner or the manager—quickly appeared and placed three thick napkins over the water-logged part of the table.

"This should take care of it, sir," she said with a reassuring smile. "Crystal, can I talk to you in the back?"

"Thanks," I said, as the owner/manager led the waitress away. Turning to my friend, I said, "Despite your protestations, it happened again, Lorenzo."

"Yeah, it happens more often than I care to admit," he sighed. "They think I'm that movie star from Spain. I've forgotten his name."

"Antonio Banderas."

"Yeah, I guess so. If these gals only knew that I swing the other way, so to speak. I think Antonio Banderas and other guys are pretty hot, myself.

"At any rate, back to the Patriot Act. No cases yet, but we want to be ready. This thing could turn into a real legal nightmare for the people caught up in it. I don't want to be an alarmist, but remember what happened during World War II when Japanese Americans were rounded up and put into camps all over the West? They were denied due process. I worry that it might happen again, but it may not be someone's ethnicity that gets them picked up. It will be because the government overhears a perfectly harmless comment—over the phone or in an e-mail or in public—and arrests the person."

"Very scary," I said. "I admire you for getting involved in this. The innocent are lucky to have you on their side. I can speak authoritatively about that."

We finished our meals and our wine.

"Some dessert?" This time, it was the older woman.

"What happened to Crystal?" I asked.

"I sent her home. She's been working too much overtime lately." She winked at both of us.

I consulted the menu. "Lorenzo?"

"Vanilla ice cream. And would you put some chocolate sauce on it?"

She nodded. "Coffee?"

"Yeah, please."

"Make it two," I said. She left, and I resumed our discussion. "You still got that cranky investigator working for you?"

"Raymond Pearl. Oh yes, Ray's still with me, but he hasn't been in the best of health lately. That hasn't helped his crankiness. He hates getting old, but I think he'll need to retire before long. He just isn't up to the job a lot of the time."

The blunt-spoken Pearl was a retired New York City cop who helped in the investigation to clear me of the murder charge. He wasn't always easy to be around, but he was effective.

"Now tell me about yourself, Thomas," said Madrid, after our ice cream had been set in front of us. "What have you been up to, besides running away from drug kingpins and going off to God knows where?"

"It's all in my book, as they say," I laughed. "I think you know a lot of it. The main thing is that Jesus Maldanado is out of business—permanently. He's dead. I suppose that his untimely end put his gang out of business, at least for now."

"That's what I heard. They left the state and are now hanging out in California with a new boss. You ever worry that one of them will come after you for being responsible for the death of their boss?"

"It's possible, but my name was kept out of all the news accounts about his demise. I was there but did not do the deed. Between you and me, someone else killed him and threw his body off the top of the Yaquina Head Lighthouse."

"I won't ask you directly, but I assume it was your friend, the army spook—Bickford is it?"

"Yeah, Paul Bickford. I better not say any more."

"What about your woman friend, Maxine? Is she still around? And are the two of you still an item?"

"No, we broke up a long time ago. It's no secret, but I won't bore you with it now. She's living in the East—New York, I think—and pursuing a new career in photography. She's off the hook too, now that Maldanado is dead."

Madrid looked at his watch. "I'd better get on the road back to Salem."

He pulled his wallet out and reached for the bill. I snatched it away before he got hold of it.

"My treat, Lorenzo. It's the least I can do. It was great to see you again. I'd like to send you a copy of my book. You are mentioned in it, of course."

"Thanks, Tom. You're making me a star."

"Yeah," I said, talking out of the corner of my mouth. "Stick with me, kid. I hope we can keep in closer touch."

"We will do just that. Count on it."

He walked out of the restaurant as I stepped to the cash register.

"Sir," said the owner/manager, "was that really that Spanish movie star?"

"Antonio Banderas. Yes, as a matter of fact, it was. He's an old friend. Actually, I'm his agent."

SPRING 2007

WHILE I WAITED FOR THE BOOK TOUR, I spent the rest of the winter holed up at home in Newport. Although I knew I needed to see people as often as possible to improve my outlook on life, I felt more comfortable by myself. I saw friends now and then, but I spent most days alone. That is, except for the workmen I hired to remodel parts of my house.

Given my negative feelings about the university commu-nity and how I felt I had been treated by most people in it, I decided to sell my condominium in Corvallis. With the hous-ing bubble yet to burst, the unit sold for double the money I had paid for it fifteen or so years ago. With the money from my book advance—and some investments—I was able to pay myself the approximate amount of my monthly pay from the univer-sity each month. I was hoping for advances for future books and royalties from the cocaine one. With the leave without pay from Oregon University, I could go back into my old position as long as I gave my chairman enough notice. I hoped I would not have to do that. I longed for the freedom a writing career would give me. It would have its own hassles and challenges, but I could, at least, control my own destiny.

With my monthly budget covered, I decided to use some of the money from the sale of my condo to do the remodeling on my Newport house. It was built well enough to withstand the harsh winds and heavy rains of the winter, but it now had a dated look. Although not the highly ridiculed shag of the 1970s, the wall-to-wall carpeting was drab and dirty in spots. When the workmen tore it up, we discovered a nice hardwood floor underneath. The kitchen was a horror, however—its metal cupboards were ugly, as was its Formica countertop. The stove, refrigerator, and dishwasher were all a bilious avocado color. It was fun to figure out a new design for this room and then order the appliances. I asked the contractor to paint the house inside and out too.

I saved the best for last: my study. I spend most of my time in this room so wanted to design it for my writing needs. I worked out a plan for a cabinetmaker to build floor-to-ceiling bookshelves on all of the walls, two built-in filing cabinets, and two large work-spaces—one for my computer and printer, the other as an area to sort and stack things and hold those old-fashioned wire baskets I use to store open files. I've always liked to have all my work in progress in plain sight.

As the men made their way methodically through the house, I spent my time cleaning out old files. It was like revisiting my past life as I read the stories I had written and built my career on. At times, I winced at both the naiveté of my thought processes and the amateurishness of my writing style. At other times, I was proud of my work and put the articles aside so I could read them again. I spent an enjoyable afternoon reading some of my favorites.

STRANGERS STOP OFF IN HOLCOMB AGAIN

For Holcomb, Kansas (population 287), fame arrived with what some residents now call "that book." Truman Capote's In Cold Blood *relates in meticulous detail the 1959 murder of the village's most prominent family: Herbert Clutter and his wife, son, and daughter. The book was published last year and 350,000 hardcover copies and two million paperbacks have been sold thus far. Since then, Holcomb hasn't been able to get away from it all. And now, the Clutter tale is about to be twice-told—this time on film by writer-director Richard Brooks (*Elmer Gantry, Cat on a Hot Tin Roof, The Blackboard Jungle, The Professionals*). Several weeks ago, Brooks moved his 70-man crew to Holcomb and two motels in nearby Garden City (population 15,000). They'll be there until May.*

ALASKAN NATIVES: EVEN HOPE IS SCARCE

The Eskimo couple had been drinking all night and now it was morning. The one-room tarpaper shack on the edge of Nome contained no conveniences. While the younger of nine children played languidly, the older ones sat about looking sullen. The Bureau of Indian Affairs official tried to converse with the couple, but their answers were unintelligible. A visitor asked the oldest son about the BIA boarding school he was attending in Oregon. He said he was anxious to return. Then he added: "I'm never coming back here again."

SUN VALLEY'S ROSIER GLOW

Habitues of Sun Valley were dismayed in 1964 when they learned that the Union Pacific Railroad was selling the famous Idaho resort. Both the railroad and Janss Corp., the big Los Angeles land developing company that bought it, were immediately flooded with letters from former guests urging that nothing be done to change Sun Valley. Said longtime resident, the actress Ann Sothern, the new construction of condos and a shopping center have ruined what she calls the "blissful isolation. It shakes you up to see cars parked where horses once ran in a field."

THE PRISON-CAMP PRACTITIONER

Maj. Floyd Kushner holds a distinction he would just as soon surrender: He is the only American military doctor to be captured during the Vietnam War. Confined in the vacuum of a Vietcong prison camp in South Vietnam since December 1967 and unaware even that doctors have succeeded in transplanting a heart, he still manages to practice medicine, according to his wife, Valerie. And she is so determined to dramatize his situation that she recently flew halfway around the world with a 17-lb. package of drugs furnished by the AMA.

CHARGE AGAINST MD: 'MURDER BY OMISSION'

From the start, the marriage was something out of a best-selling novel-turned-tear-jerking motion picture: Rich society girl marries handsome medical student from poor background and helps him become famous plastic surgeon. The fictional version always had a happy ending. The real thing did not.

LEGENDARY 'DR. KARL' WELL INFORMED, ACTIVE AT 76

He speaks from the vantage point of years of experience, but he does not live in the past. He remains the grand old man of psychiatry. Yet nobody consults Dr. Karl Menninger much any more about how to run the organization he helped found in 1925 and now serves as board chairman. "Dr. Karl" now refers all questions to his nephew, Roy, president.

SKYJACKED MD HELPED CAPTIVES
FIGHT DESPAIR IN THE DESERT

The desert sun beating against the aluminum skin of the Swissair DC-8 pushed temperatures inside the aircraft to as high as 105 degrees. The wind outside only stirred up a dust storm. And the smell from clogged toilets permeated the stale air inside the plane. Mothers strained in this suffocating atmosphere to amuse children lest they cry and captors take them away. The situation on that baked-clay, dry-lake landing strip in the Jordanian desert, where three hijacked jetliners and hundreds of passengers were held for a week last month by Palestinian guerrillas, was patently miserable. But for one of the two American doctors involved, it never became as critical as it might have been.

'WOULD YOU WANT YOUR DAUGHTER
TO MARRY A GP?'

It was after 5 p.m. and his day off, but Dr. James G. Price was seeing a patient. The Brush, Colorado, general practitioner gets calls at home every night of the week. This one had been from the mother of a 16-year-old girl who had stubbed her toe several days earlier, injuring the nail, which she had then clipped too closely. "Sure, bring her right over," he said, as he stood in the doorway between his patio and kitchen.

Dr. Price's evening chores exemplify both the good and the bad of being a small-town GP today.

EMERGENCY DEPARTMENTS AND
THE NON-EMERGENCY DELUGE

Patients who walk into the emergency department of Cook County Hospital in Chicago must pass a large statue of a mother comforting her children and protecting them from unseen dangers.

That art nouveau reminder of the hospital's palmier days is a bit of grandeur largely missing inside the old institution now. But the image of protection and aid the statue symbolically offers is taken quite seriously by those who see it. Last year, 214,000 people used the adult emergency department.

ANOTHER HUGHES 'SECRET'—
HIS VAST MEDICAL ENTERPRISE

On the surface, there is little of medical interest about Howard Hughes except the recently reported decline in his own health. The reclusive billionaire spends thousands each year waging a reverse public relations campaign to keep news of his personal life and enterprises out of the media. This effort, plus his own inaccessibility (the picture with this article was taken in 1946), holds authoritative information to a minimum and leaves the man and his works open to wild speculation. The speculation extends even to Hughes's philanthropic works, for below the surface, there is much medical interest in the man. Buried in the complex organizational charts of his $2 billion empire is the Howard Hughes Medical Institute in Miami. And the measures he has taken to protect it from publicity are almost as extensive as those cloaking Hughes himself, leading the casual observer to question the worth of its work and the high-mindedness of its objectives. The reason, of course, lies in its sole benefactor.

MEDICINE BEHIND BARS:
HOSTILITY, HORROR, AND THE HIPPOCRATIC OATH

It isn't easy to be a physician in a prison. Working behind bars, a doctor must watch every pill given to an inmate to make sure that he swallows it and does not tongue it and try to sell it later to give a fellow inmate a slight "high." He must carefully control the dispensing of drugs and disposable syringes and needles and hold the staff accountable for each item. He must be able to tell when an inmate is sick and when he is malingering to get out of work. He must deal with correctional officers to make sure that prisoners who need medical help are not denied it for arbitrary and punitive reasons, and he must be sure that inmate-workers are not blackmailed into granting special favors to others.

"A lot of doctors get involved in prison work because they can't hack it any place else," said a former prison physician now in private practice. "Their self-image isn't good."

DENIZENS OF THE DEEP

April—The Bering Strait. The bowhead whales have been gathering for several weeks, waiting for the ice pack to break up. The leads in the ice that open will form the natural corridor along which the whales will migrate through the Chukchi Sea and into the Beaufort Sea, their summer feeding area.

Instinct tells them to form for the journey as they have for centuries, perhaps as long ago as the time just after Alaska and Siberia were linked by a solid land bridge. Ahead on the journey are possible perils, old and new.

I put the files back into boxes and sat for a while contemplating my career in journalism. While no president had resigned or foreign government had fallen or movie star had been ruined by anything I wrote, I was proud of the work I had done. By working in New York— then as now the epicenter of American journalism—the old "if you can make it here, you can make it anywhere" dictum applied. I had reached the top of my profession. I loved the travel and the reporting and the writing. I was less enamored with living in Manhattan because of the expense, the huge number of people everywhere, and the difficulty of doing even the simplest of daily tasks. I had left New York for the halls of the university and had been happy there. For twenty years I had never looked back—until now. It seemed, at first glance anyway, that these pieces and some new ones might make an interesting book, especially if I included the background to each story.

On this rainy afternoon, I next turned my attention to my books. I had once counted them and now updated the list every time I bought a new one. I had over 2,000 books, and I bought most of them for a reason—either I needed them for research or I wanted to read them. Thus, it was hard to figure out which ones to discard. I have always loved books and never loaned my copies to anyone. If you do that, you never get them back. I would rather buy someone a book than give them one of mine. With new bookshelves on the way, I finally decided I would keep most of these, although I set aside a few old textbooks to take to the library for its weekly book sale.

As the work on the house neared completion, I took a trip to Ashland to see several Shakespeare plays. I figured I needed to be out of the way while the work in my office was done.

On that trip, while I stayed in a hotel near the Elizabethan theatre downtown, I mapped out my plans for the summer, which would be one of traveling to book events and revising my old articles. When I got back, I called my agent to tell her about my idea for the collection. She was immediately enthusiastic.

"I think I can sell them on the idea that the book would be an ideal adjunct to *The Cocaine Trail*," she said. "Usually collections— whether they be short stories by a novelist or articles by a nonfiction writer—are dead in the water. But this would fly with a modest printing, and maybe we could even get it adopted by some journalism professors. Maybe you'd even adopt it."

I laughed. I hoped never to see the inside of a classroom again.

"Sure, I could see it being adopted as a secondary text, if it was in paperback. Textbooks are so costly now that kids have a tough time buying their primary books, let alone one that is supplemental."

"I can pitch it as that, but the decision on hardcover or paperback is not one we can make," she said.

Janet submitted the proposal and, after a week, the publisher bought it and gave me another contract. This time, however, there was no advance.

I was now in the process of selecting the old articles to go into the book and writing the background to each one. I had also decided on two new ones: one on Lorenzo Madrid, my former lawyer, and one on Michaela Ross, my new cellist friend.

As I sat in my newly refurbished office, I felt more confident and at peace than I had in a long time.

SUMMER 2007

THE REVISIONS OF THE OLDER ARTICLES had taken longer than I expected, but I was now ready to start working on the profiles of both Michaela and Lorenzo. Since Michaela lived closer, I started with her.

In June, I attended a rehearsal of the symphony orchestra at Michaela's invitation. The musicians were already milling around on stage when I walked into the rear of the auditorium where the rehearsal would take place. The orchestra did not have a permanent home, so they had to perform in a variety of venues over the years.

This one was an old grade school that had been turned into a cultural center. Just stepping inside brought back memories of my own grammar school days in California; the sight of faded paint on the walls and worn linoleum and the smells of chalk and mustiness brought back things I had long since forgotten.

Michaela broke away from talking to a short, blond woman when she saw me come in. She walked to the side of the stage and down the few steps to the floor and then up the aisle to where I was sitting.

"Hi, Tom. Glad you could make it."

"I wanted to see you in action, Mike. Maybe you can fill me in later on the intricacies of how the orchestra operates."

"There won't be much magic with this guy in charge," she said, shaking her head in dismay. "He is certifiably nuts. A maniac who does not really know a B flat from an F minor."

"Do other members feel the same way?"

"All except that blond cutie I was talking to. She's the second cello—brought up from the rear by this guy after she bleached her hair blond to be noticed. She does not have the experience to be where she is, but our 'august' conductor, Mr. Horatio Pine, loves playing footsie with her, so here she is. I know she is gunning for my job, and she may well get it unless I can figure out how to stop her. The competition for these slots is tremendous because we are the only game in town. Dear Horatio tried to get me into bed last year, but I wouldn't do it. I laughed in his face when he made a pass at me in the basement of this very hall."

"Not a good career move," I laughed.

"I have faith in my ability, and I certainly don't need sex to get ahead." She turned to glance at the stage. "There's the little creep now. I'd better go."

She turned to walk down the aisle, then paused. "Oh, I almost forgot . . . I told him about you being here and made it sound as if your article would be about the orchestra. He's probably thinking that it will be about him since, in his mind, *he* is the orchestra. He won't bother you, but he might come over so you can jot down his words of wisdom."

With that, Michaela turned and walked down to the side stairs and up onto the stage. The maestro watched her coming and then turned to me. He nodded his head, then turned to the music arrayed in front of him on the podium. Horatio Pine was short and a bit rotund. He looked taller than he was because of his immense head of hair, which probably stood up at least five inches. This accouterment made him look like a cross between the notorious fight promoter Don King and the *New Yorker* writer Malcolm Gladwell.

Pine glanced around the stage, then tapped his baton on the podium. At first, the musicians ignored his gentle tap. They kept talking and tuning their instruments, creating a deafening cacophony.

More tapping.

More ignoring.

He then nodded to the diminutive woman who was, I guess, first violin. She stood up, put two fingers inside her mouth, and whistled as though to attract the attention of a bunch of dock workers or army recruits. The musicians quit playing and talking and turned their attention to Mr. Pine.

"Thank you, Karen, for that valuable and timely assist," he said to her, a big smile on his face. Then turning to everyone, he said, "Okay, people. I don't have to tell you that we have less than a month to get ready for our big Fourth of July concert at the Coast Guard station in Newport. We will need to rehearse twice a week, starting next week."

There were groans from the players.

"We've got other jobs," said one of the percussionists.

"We've got other commitments," said a trumpeter.

"I shouldn't have to remind you that I expect your commitment to this orchestra to come first in your life," said Pine, nodding to himself as if to validate the truth of his statement.

"Jesus H. Christ," said a bass player, a tall man with a pony tail. "It is very easy for you to say that. You are the only one of us here who makes a regular salary—$15,000 a year for four concerts, I think it is."

There were gasps from the others as if they were hearing the figure for the first time.

"I don't think my salary should be public knowledge," said Pine defensively. "You fail to remember that I was the one who went to the board and got pay for all of you." He nodded again, his wild hair moving in the breeze that motion created.

"This fighting is getting us nowhere," said the blond woman sitting next to Michaela. "We have to get ready for our performance. The show must go on and all of that stuff."

"The show could easily go on without your sour notes," said the bass player. "We all know why you got to be second cello, don't we."

The woman began dabbing at her eyes. Pine seemed to be at a loss for words. He became busy consulting the musical score on the podium in front of him.

"We will, of course, be playing the *1812 Overture* by Pyotr Ilyich Tchaikovsky," said Pine. "It is a traditional piece to play on the Fourth of July, and I have arranged for a detachment from the Oregon National Guard to fire a big gun from the state park above the Yaquina Bay Bridge at the appropriate point in the music. I should say that Monk Beasley, the officer in charge of the Coast Guard station at Newport, has arranged for the gun. I am coordinating this whole program with him. We'll be playing from the grounds of the station there on the other side of the bridge."

I was impressed that Pine had known who to contact. Beasley was a good friend of mine. I attended the open house he held very year on the Fourth of July and enjoyed the view of the fireworks from the front porch of the headquarters building overlooking the bay and bridge. I knew he would make sure that this program went off smoothly.

The members of the orchestra seemed pleased with the plans Pine had made. Maybe he wasn't as bad as Michaela had said.

"We'll get to Mr. Tchaikovsky in a moment. We will be playing another selection. I'd like to begin with a run-through of our opening piece, Beethoven's *Fifth Symphony*."

There were more moans from the musicians.

"That old chestnut," muttered someone.

"I know it by heart," said another, "and I don't want to know it at all."

For me, listening to it was a pleasure. I don't know a lot about classical music, but I do like familiar works by the old masters. When I go to concerts, I search the program immediately to see what works are scheduled to be played. Any composer still alive or born in the twentieth century will have written compositions that sound awful. They may be challenging for the musicians to play and a way for an orchestra to expand the knowledge of an audience, but they are hell on the ears. As I sat in the drafty concert hall, the familiar sound of *Da da da dum* was reassuring.

Very quickly into the piece, the orchestra seemed to be going in several directions. Horns were coming in at the wrong time and violins had seemingly gone off on their own. At the podium, Horatio Pine seemed oblivious to the meandering musicians before him. As Michaela said he might, he had gotten lost. After a few more seconds, he started paging through the sheets of music on the stand. Before long, various pages began falling to the floor.

At this point, Karen, the first violinist and, I presume, concertmaster, stood up and whistled again—this time more loudly than before. The musicians immediately stopped playing.

I recalled what Michaela had said about the accepted way for a conductor to work. She said he or she should rule the orchestra, setting the tempo and creating the sound. "The conductor is the boss," she had said. At this moment, Pine was very far from that.

The violinist walked over and began to pick up the sheets of music from the floor. Michaela soon joined her and began arranging the pages in order. Pine busied himself with examining his fingernails and patting his unruly hair. Karen handed him the pages, but he barely acknowledged her in accepting them.

"Aren't you even going to say thank you, Mr. Pine?" yelled the big bass player with the ponytail. "Jesus H. Christ."

Other players mumbled their agreement, but no one else spoke aloud until the small blond cellist sitting next to Michaela stood up.

"You are being hateful toward Horatio!" she screamed. "He does so much for all of us—how can you treat him this way? And you are the worst!" She turned to Michaela next to her. "You have created a climate of mistrust for both him and me!"

Michaela looked baffled. With all eyes trained on her, she stood up.

"I don't know what you're talking about, Sheila. All I know is that a while back you bleached your hair so that Horatio would notice you, and I guess it worked because you're now second cello, and you're sleeping with him. Should we all bleach our hair blond?"

At that point, Sheila slapped Michaela and started pulling her hair. I rose from my seat hesitatingly because, as a guest, I had no right to get involved. I was saved by the bass player, who pulled Sheila away from Michaela and led her off the stage. For his part, Pine was still gazing at the music in front of him. After a few seconds, he looked up and tapped his baton.

"Let us begin again."

And they did.

Da da da dum.

WHILE I WAITED FOR THE FOURTH OF JULY CONCERT, I decided to turn to the piece I planned to write about Lorenzo Madrid. Madrid's office was in an old house located on the unfashionable northeast side of Salem, Oregon's capital. Most state buildings surrounded the mall near downtown. The better residential areas lay south and west of there.

In Madrid's part of town, the people looked decidedly unprosperous. Men and women on the streets had the faded, vacant-eyed look of people who had not been out in the sun for a while—maybe had been living in the state mental hospital or one of several prisons located in town.

Here was where Hispanics lived too, both legally and illegally. These law-abiding people made up Madrid's regular clientele, although some were always on the verge of deportation.

Lorenzo represented them for little or no money. He supplemented the meager state and federal funds available to help those people by taking high-profile cases for which he charged the high fees his skill commanded. He was much in demand, especially from rich ladies in trouble over minor infractions of the law or in need of large divorce settlements to pay for their exorbitant lifestyles.

Because it was after hours, the waiting room was empty. As I closed the door, I could hear loud voices from the rear.

"Damn right, I don't want to retire! You need me, and I need the money!"

"Ray, you just can't maintain the pace you once did. You've got to face the fact that it's time to retire."

I could tell that Lorenzo was talking to his investigator, Raymond Pearl. This gruff, profane man was skilled at what he did, but Lorenzo had told me he was in poor health and slowing down. Obviously, he was not ready to admit it.

"Tom," said Lorenzo from his office. "Come on back."

I walked down the hall and into the room where the men were standing.

"You remember Ray Pearl."

"You bet I do. Hi Ray."

I reached out my hand to shake his, but the older man only glared at me. He had not changed. He still looked like a broken-down prizefighter with a nose that was slightly off-kilter and a red face that was deeply lined. He still wore his hair in a massive comb-over that was plastered down with so much hair oil that it probably would not have moved even in a hurricane.

The contrast to the handsome Madrid was striking. Even dressed in jeans and a blue work shirt, Lorenzo still looked like Banderas, the movie star.

"Ray and I were just talking about his retirement, right?"

Pearl mumbled something that sounded like "shit" but said nothing else.

"I was just telling him that he should write his memoirs. He's got lots of stories. Right, Ray?"

"Damn you, Lorenzo," said Pearl, in a loud voice. "Don't do this to me in front of someone else. Why are you humiliating me?"

"Tom's a friend, and I'm not humiliating you. I'm just talking sense. Your health isn't as good as it used to be. You can't take the long days and the late hours. You're forgetting things."

As if on cue, Pearl started to cough—a deep, wheezing cough that racked his body for several minutes. Lorenzo poured a glass of water and handed it to Pearl, who quickly drank it.

"Enough said. You've made my point for me. Think about what I said, and we'll talk in the morning."

He got up and walked over to Pearl and helped him stand up. The older man at first tried to push Lorenzo's arm away, but then seemed to decide he needed it and grabbed hold.

"I just don't want to lose this job. It's all I got, Lorenzo, you damn Latin heartthrob."

Then the two men hugged, and Madrid walked him through the door and down the hall. I heard a short exchange of words and then the front door opening and closing.

"I hated to do that to Ray, but I thought it might embarrass him enough to retire if I talked about the situation in front of you," Lorenzo said, as he sat down behind his desk. "He just doesn't have the skills he once had, and I need someone who knows the law and can do research on the Internet. Investigative work is no longer a job where you sit out in front of someone's house all night, waiting to see who climbs out the window. Coffee?"

"Yeah, please. Black."

Madrid poured me a cup from the pot sitting on a shelf behind his desk, then continued.

"Another thing: he's pretty rough around the edges and swears a lot. That may have worked well when he was a New York cop, but it rubs people around here the wrong way. Oregonians don't swear a lot or have foul mouths."

"What'll you do without him?"

"I do a lot of this myself already. Plus I get help from law students at Willamette University. They like the experience and the money. Also, I might turn to investigative reporters like you, Tom."

Lorenzo smiled and winked in a way that I could not judge whether he was serious or just kidding. I did not respond.

"Okay, let's get to the third degree you're going to put me through. For a preening, conceited attorney, I really don't like to talk about myself. I'm only doing this for you. What do you want to know?"

I pulled out my notebook and a list of questions I had prepared. "I do want to observe you in action in court and also when you interact with clients—if that's allowed without violating confidentially."

"I think that can be arranged," he said.

"Before that, I want to get some personal stuff out of the way."

"Great. That's easy enough. I was born in East L.A. to a family of Mexican migrants who had come to the United States through the *bracero* program in the 1950s and 1960s. At that time, the farmers in California were allowed to bring workers in legally to harvest crops. My father came and worked for a few years up in the San Joaquin Valley and met my mother, who was born in the United States. They got married and moved down to L.A., where he started a nursery business and did well. I am the baby of the family, with two married sisters who are both teachers. That is my background in a nutshell."

He paused to sip more coffee.

"Is this the kind of stuff you want?"

I nodded.

"So, where did you go to college?

"UCLA—right out of high school on an academic scholarship."

"You were what other kids called 'a brain'?"

"You bet I was—all through grammar school and junior high, this little brown kid who knew all the answers and got beat up all the time for knowing them. But I started getting taller and fighting back, so the mean kids began to leave me alone."

"Law school next, after your B.A.?"

"Yes, at Cal in Berkeley. Another full-ride scholarship."

"Did you aspire to leave the barrio behind and work in one of those big buildings you no doubt could see from East L.A.?"

"For a while I did, but something happened to me and a friend of mine that changed my mind and got me into public service law. Now I try to help people who need me."

"Can you tell me what happened?"

"Sure, I'll give you the whole sordid tale. It revolves around my being gay. I hinted at that when I came to your book signing and we had dinner. I want that fact to be very clear in your article. Is that acceptable?"

"It is," I said. "I wanted to get into that subject, but I wasn't sure how."

"Tom, it is a part of me, and long ago I learned not to hide it. I 'fought the good fight' against what I once considered a shameful thing until this incident happened that I mentioned earlier. It brought me out of the closet and into practicing the kind of law I love."

"I'm ready to listen," I said. "Would you like me to stop taking notes?"

"Yeah, maybe it would be less intimidating for now."

I put down my pen and nodded.

"As I said, I fought against the thought that I might be gay all through school and into college. Even though I was bookish and not very good at sports, I was able to hide my tendency to gaze amorously at boys in the shower room instead of girls' boobs at the senior prom. This was hard to do in the macho world I grew up in. It helped that I was the baby in a family of two sisters who doted on me. My parents were kind and loving and tried to help me succeed at whatever I wanted to do. I owe them everything."

Lorenzo's eyes filled with tears at the memory. "Sorry. They both died too young. From all that hard work, I think."

I nodded but kept quiet so I wouldn't intrude on his grief.

"Okay then, let me begin. I met a guy when I was at UCLA, an

Anglo guy. Scott was about as white as they come—blond, blue-eyed, very preppy looking. He came from a wealthy family in Pasadena, just over the hills from East L.A. but as different as another planet in terms of lifestyle, wealth, and the kind of people who live there. We met in a sociology class and started going out for coffee after class. To him, I was at first a subject to be studied. He wanted to be a social worker in the very kind of community I was trying to escape from. He wanted to know all about me and my family.

"Before long, the discussions became more personal, and we both revealed that we were gay—maybe the first time either of us had done so to another person. Until then, I had gone to great lengths to conceal my deepest secret, and now I found myself pouring out all the pent-up frustrations and humiliations I had encountered my entire life. He did the same, telling me about growing up with two brothers who were jocks and very abusive toward him because he had always been so different. His father often joined in the ridicule and his mother, although sympathetic, never took his side. He could not get away from that hostile environment soon enough."

Lorenzo stopped talking to take a sip of coffee. He gazed out the window at the streetlight as if to collect his thoughts.

"This is hard. I haven't thought about any of this for a while."

"Take your time," I said.

"Scott decided to major in social work instead of law or medicine like his father tried to push him into. And that's why he came to UCLA and we met. He allowed me to become his touchstone, the one person who could understand him both personally and professionally."

"I assume you two became lovers?"

"Not right away. It took about a month of nearly daily coffee dates and late-night gab sessions, where he asked me all kinds of questions about where I lived and the people and what they went through. I was able to suggest people in the neighborhood who would be good sources for him. I mean, I had lived with them all my life. That is what I meant about being a *professional* touchstone. One night after I had known him for a month, he became distraught over how badly his family had treated him, and we just fell into each other's arms. I couldn't relate because my family had been so good to me. But I had been teased over my occasional effeminate ways by kids in the neighborhood."

"That's hard to believe, Lorenzo," I said. "I mean, you are so—how can I put this—masculine now."

"Well, I guess I am, and it's not all an act. I couldn't do my job here if I pranced around in lavender pants and a gold lame tank top."

We both smiled at the thought.

"So we became lovers and were both happy for about six months. During that time, I went home for visits once in a while because I missed my folks and my sisters. My mother sensed that I was happy, so she asked me if I had a special friend, and I told her about Scott. She took the news fairly well but wondered how my father would react. As we were talking about it, he walked into the room.

" 'React to what?' he asked. So I told him about Scott, and he became enraged and hit me. 'No son of mine is going to be a fairy.' That kind of thing. He got so upset, in fact, that he had a heart attack right there in front of us. We rushed him to the hospital, and he was in critical condition for a week. Even though he got better, it was clear to me that he would never be able to run the nursery again. So, I dropped out of school for the rest of the semester. I moved home and took over the running of the business. I had no choice. My dad had no medical insurance, and my mother did not work. They had no income except for the nursery. My sisters were gone by then."

"What about Scott?"

"We kept in touch by phone almost daily. He wanted to see me but I warned him against coming to East L.A. I knew with his blond hair and white face and sports car, he would be an instant target.

After a month, I really needed to be with him, so I relented and told him how to find the nursery. I told my mother that I was going to stay late and work on the books. Scott arrived at about 9 p.m., and we immediately embraced, right there in the office.

"Unfortunately, Enrique, the kid who watered the plants, picked that night to come back to get a school book he had left in his locker. He was a good worker and not a bad kid, but he was a gang wannabe—not a member, but he thought it was neat to hang out with tough guys. When he saw us rolling around on the couch in the office, he started yelling *maricón*—that means queer—at the top of his lungs. He ran out into the street and whistled. In seconds, the office was full of gangbangers. Scott and I were vulnerable, lying there naked without so much as a sheet to cover us.

"Their leader, a real punk named Eduardo, walked over to us and started laughing. Then he and the others started kicking us with their steel-toed boots. They singled out Scott because he was Caucasian. As two of them dragged me out of the way and held me, they beat him and cut his body repeatedly. I yelled until I was hoarse but could do nothing to stop them. After about ten minutes, Scott fainted, and they threw him into the corner. Then they spit on him.

"Eduardo turned to me and signaled the others to release my arms. He went on and on about how I had sold out my people by getting involved with a white guy and that I would get what was coming to me if I kept this up, etc., etc. Oddly, he did not hit me again. At his signal, the others filed out of the room, including the hapless Enrique who had started it all. When they were gone, I staggered over to Scott and discovered that he had no pulse. He was dead."

"My God, Lorenzo. I am so sorry," I said.

Lorenzo became very pale. Dredging up the long-repressed story was almost more than he could bear, even this many years later.

"We can finish this some other time," I said to break the silence.

"No, no. I need to get it off my chest. It will help you understand me."

"What did you do?"

"I called the police and waited until they arrived. I put on my clothes but left Scott exactly as they had left him. After some fairly hostile questions, the detectives assigned to the case began to believe me. With my help, they arrested all of the gang members, including Eduardo and Enrique. I testified against them, after selling the nursery and moving my parents out of East L.A. to the west side of town near campus."

"What about Scott's parents and brothers?"

"Only his mother attended the trial, and we never exchanged anything more than a few glances in the courtroom. They blamed me for his death and would not let me attend his funeral.

"From that day forward, I vowed to seek justice in the world. I vowed to make sure that no bad deed would go unpunished. I went to law school and decided to help those who no one else would help—brown, black, white. Ironically, Scott was not among the downtrodden in terms of the unserved people I wound up representing. But he was someone whose death might not have been avenged had I not testified against his killers. I needed justice to be done for him, and that has carried over into the career path I have followed. As corny as it sounds, I decided that night to work tirelessly for justice. And, to get real personal on you here, Tom, I have done it alone. I have not had a lover since Scott died."

He looked at me with tears in his eyes.

"God, I am so sorry about what happened to you. I can't begin to understand your loss, and to have it happen in front of you is unfathomable. I don't know what to say. I want to be your friend and sometime client, but I don't . . ."

"Are you worried that I am hitting on you?" he said, wiping his eyes. "I just needed someone to listen to my tale of woe, and you need material to use in your article. I mean it when I said that I have been going through life alone. I have no desire to have sex with anyone, believe me."

"This is awkward," I said. "I shouldn't have presumed that you were interested in me. I just thought I should clear the air and tell you where I stand."

"Point taken," he replied. "I think it is always good for friends to know where they stand with each other."

"I need to ask you how you want to handle all of this in my article. I think it will strengthen your story and the theme that I am thinking of following—justice for the downtrodden—if I include some of what happened with Scott. But if it is too painful, we can leave it out. Your emergence from the barrio is enough of a theme to build on, even without the story of you and Scott. And won't that dredge up a lot of bad stuff with you and your parents?"

"Too late for that. My dad died a year later, literally of a broken heart. He never looked at me the same way again after that night. And I felt tremendous guilt that what I had done—revealing the fact that I was gay—had killed him. My mom died two years later. So, I am quite alone, except for my sisters and their families, and because they are married and have different last names, I feel I am able to tell my story without hurting them."

We talked for another hour, and I jotted down some of what he told me after I got into my car. Then I drove back to the coast, my head full of the makings of a great story, but one tinged with a good friend's agony.

JULY 4, 2007

I DROVE MICHAELA TO THE FOURTH OF JULY CONCERT.
I planned to observe the members of the orchestra as they got set
up and rehearsed.

"I think you already know we'll be playing that old Fourth of
July standard, Tchaikovsky's *1812 Overture*," she said, as we pulled
away from her house.

"Guns and all?"

"Guns and all," she laughed. "Horatio said the other day that he
has arranged with an artillery unit to bring over a couple of howitzers to lob some dummy shells into Yaquina Bay in a synchronous
fashion in time with the music. You'll remember that it's part of the
big finish of that piece."

"Oh yeah, I've always loved it. I've seen it in New York and
Boston. It is wonderful."

"As I'm sure you know, Tchaikovsky wrote it to commemorate
Napoleon's retreat from Moscow in 1812. It has everything—the
guns of battle, the church bells of victory, even a bit of *La Marseillaise*.
Cellists love it because it begins with what I call a cello choir in a

part called 'Hail to the Czar.' Then the violas come in and off we go. After that, I hate performing it because it has a million notes. The way he wrote it, there is scale after scale after scale. I've gotten to the point where I can play it with my eyes closed, but you can't do that because people know the piece so well, they will notice if you make a mistake. And there are traps that are tricky so you have to stay alert."

We were making the turn off Highway 101 by this time and driving under the Yaquina Bay Bridge. I knew this road well because of my years on the lighthouse friends' group board. I headed down the hill and around to the rear service gate of the Coast Guard station, at the bottom where we would park.

"Thanks for the background, Mike. I'll need to write it down so I won't forget it. You're very quotable."

"I've been called many things, but 'quotable' has never been one of them," she said with a laugh. "Just pull over there—I've got a parking pass to put on the dashboard."

As I pulled through the gate, a young coastguardsman appeared.

"Evening, sir." He leaned down and looked across to Michaela. "Ma'am."

"This lady is a member of the orchestra, and I am her driver," I said.

Michaela handed the parking pass over to him. He glanced at it and handed it back to her.

"Excellent, ma'am. Just pull over there next to that Jeep. Parking's pretty tight so it may take a while to sort this out at the end of the concert."

"No problem," I said. "We won't be in any hurry."

I drove the car to the spot he indicated, and we got out. I walked around to the rear and opened the trunk. Michaela reached in to pull out the large case holding her cello. I leaned in to help her, but she waved me off.

"When you've hefted this thing as long as I have, it's a piece of cake. And I need to keep my arm muscles in tone, but thanks for offering."

"I think we go up that way," I said, pointing up the hill to the buildings at the top.

We walked up some stairs and across the grass in front of the main building of the Coast Guard station. I could see the orchestra setting up at the other end, in front of the barracks building.

"I'm glad it's nice and warm and dry tonight," she said, looking up at the sky. "Dampness is hard on our instruments."

We stopped walking and she turned to me.

"Tom, thanks for driving me here. I need to go over some of the music with my fellow cellists now. Sit as close as you can and observe, and I will fill you in afterward on anything you need to know."

She walked toward the assembling musicians, greeting many with slaps on their backs and hearty handshakes. I could tell that her good humor made Michaela a favorite among her fellow players.

I saw the man Michaela said would be responsible for making sure the gunners came in on cue. I found his name in my notes: Ted May. He was wearing a headset and had the score of the music arrayed in front of him on a stand. Another man dressed in army fatigues was pointing at the music and then at an area on the other side of the bridge. I followed his outstretched arm and saw three guns in place in a parking area near the entrance to the park.

The Yaquina Bay Lighthouse is surrounded by a state park. Although older by one year and not as well known as its sister structure a few miles up the coast, the Yaquina Head Lighthouse, the bay lighthouse is a popular tourist attraction. For one thing, it is right off Highway 101; for another, admission is free. The building itself is not all that impressive. It looks like an 1870s-style house with a fairly modest light tower on top. Indeed, its construction in 1871 had been largely a waste of money because its relatively modest height meant that ships trying to find its light as a guide to enter Yaquina Bay often missed it. The lighthouse on the Head, on the other hand, is Oregon's tallest, and its light is visible from far out at sea. It was completed in 1873.

As I looked at the guns in place, my eyes settled on the bridge above. It would make a majestic backdrop for the concert. Finished in 1936 as one in a series of five bridges built to replace ferries along what was then called the Pacific Coast Highway, this magnificent steel span was designed by C. B. McCullough, the longtime chief highway engineer of the Oregon Highway Department. From 1919 to 1936, he designed hundreds of bridges all over the state. I knew all of this because the man had once taught civil engineering at my college, and I had written an article about him for the alumni magazine.

Because the country and the state were then deep into the Great Depression, the state proposed that the bridges be built of wood, in order to give the struggling timber industry an economic boost. McCullough fought this idea for two reasons: the harsh weather would be hard on the wood both in maintenance and durability; also, the federal Works Progress Administration would not provide funding for any structure not made of strong materials. The engineer got his way, and the bridges were made of concrete and steel. In the years since, only the bridge over the Alsea River at Waldport has had to be replaced.

I have always been a fan of anything from the 1930s, whether it be styles of clothing or artwork or bridge design. McCullough built his bridges so that motorists driving over them felt safe. This philosophy led him to make them huge with arch-shaped structures you can see from far away. He placed pylons and obelisks at the ends of the structures—some tall and stately, others short and stumpy. Another characteristic of McCullough bridges was putting Gothic or Romanesque arches underneath, which gave them the beauty of a Roman aqueduct.

I turned away from this scene and walked back up the hill to the headquarters building. There on the long veranda was one of my closest friends Monk Beasley, the commander of this Coast Guard station. As I had been on several Fourth of July celebrations in the past, I was his guest for the evening. He and his wife, Linda, always hosted the men and women of the station and their spouses and children, along with people he invited from the town.

"Hi, Monk. Are you ready for the big show?"

"Tom, so good to see you. How've you been?"

"Not bad, Monk. I seem to be in control of my various demons, at the moment anyway. I'm writing again, and that always puts me in a good frame of mind."

"Glad to hear it," Monk said, giving me a big hug like he always does when we see each other. "You have been through more in the past year than most people encounter in a lifetime."

Monk had rescued me from the drug gang by letting me hide at his house, then getting me on a media tour of the Arctic. I knew I could always count on his help.

"I still worry about you, Tom. I worry that you will fall into a PTSD hole. I was there myself once, and it's no fun."

I appreciated his concern, but this was not the time to tell him about my nightmares.

"I'm fine, Monk. Really. Now, what've you got for us tonight? A really big show, I'll bet."

Monk beamed at the question. After a career of helping people in big ways—like saving them from drowning when their boat capsized—he loved to provide them with smaller, fun stuff, like a Fourth of July party to watch a fireworks display and listen to good music.

"Along with our usual hot dog extravaganza, we've got the best view of the fireworks across the bay," he said, spreading his arms to encompass the scene in front of us, with the setting sun shining on the sparkling waters of Yaquina Bay where small boats bobbed in the gentle current. "And how about having the symphony serenade us? I think that is really neat."

"Me too, Monk. Was it your idea?"

"Yeah, kind of. They always play in the community center, but I thought it would be better if this year they joined us out here so more people could hear them. I had to sign in blood that it would not rain."

"Yeah, dampness can really be hard on their instruments."

"It's not only been rain-less but also dry," he continued. "I promised the conductor—Horatio something, like Horatio Hornblower, the fictional sea captain I read about as a kid. An odd duck, really strange acting. Actually, I dealt more with the assistant conductor, guy named Ted May." Monk gestured toward where the orchestra was gathering and taking their seats. "He's there with the headset. He'll cue the army to shoot the guns at the proper time. Ever hear the *1812 Overture*, Tom?"

"Yes, many times. It's always been one of my favorites."

Monk looked at his clipboard and his watch. "I've got to get moving. Still have a lot of things to do before showtime. Help yourself to food. Linda's inside supervising everyone. I'll see you when the program begins."

"Thanks for everything, Monk. I'll entertain myself."

As he walked in front of the building, I turned toward the bay and took a deep breath. This was one of those times when that I was glad I lived on the Oregon coast. Nothing matches the sea air for clearing your head or calming your soul. In moments like this, coastal residents forget about the rain and wind of winter.

I walked back toward where the orchestra was getting organized. I wanted to observe the process so I could include descriptions of it in my article about Michaela. She saw me approach and motioned to me to join her. She was talking to the assistant conductor.

"Tom Martindale, this is Ted May, our second in command. He'll be calling the shots tonight, so to speak."

May, a nice-looking guy with a neatly trimmed red beard, shook my hand. I could smell alcohol on his breath.

"Always good to meet a friend of Michaela's because she has so few friends," he said, a deadpan look on his face.

She burst into a loud guffaw and slapped him on the back.

"She tells me you're writing an article about her," he continued. "That's great."

"Yes, that's right. I'm here to listen to good music and to see how the orchestra works behind the scenes. I'm especially interested in how you'll coordinate the firing of the guns," I said, gesturing toward the howitzers on the other side of the bridge.

May started to answer, then stopped. His face hardened as he looked behind me. "That dirty son of a bitch." He rushed around me toward two people walking on the opposite side the orchestra area.

Michaela shook her head. "Poor guy. That's May's former wife, Sheila Cross. In the words of my beloved grandmother, she 'stepped out on him' with Horatio Pine. She's really flaunting her access, if you get my meaning."

I recognized Sheila as the blond woman who had gotten into the hair-pulling match with Michaela at the rehearsal. She was smiling as she walked arm in arm with the wild-haired conductor, gazing into his face with sheer adulation. They both stopped in their tracks when Ted May reached them.

Members of the orchestra stopped tuning their instruments to watch.

May took a swing at Pine, and Sheila screamed. Fortunately for all, he missed and fell into a music stand, which clattered to the ground. May's inebriation made it difficult for him to get back on his feet. He grasped at another music stand and it, too, collapsed. Pine all but cowered behind Sheila, who was shouting at May.

"You tried to kill Horatio! You are crazy! I'll never speak to you again! I never loved you!"

The scene was painful to watch. I started walking over to help Ted May up, but the big bass player with the ponytail got there before me. The now sobbing man accepted the arm of his friend and struggled to his feet.

"Sheila, don't say that! We loved each other. We made plans to have a family. We were going to spend our . . ."

"I never want to see you again," she shouted, letting the still frightened Horatio Pine put his head on her shoulder.

The bass player led May away from them toward where Michaela and I were standing. When they reached us, she quickly took over as May sat down looking dejected.

"Ted, she's not worth it," said Michaela, as she kneeled in front of him. "Just forget her."

"That's hard to do when I have to see her every day—see her with that creep."

"Let me help you get another job. I've got good friends with the symphony in Walla Walla. You're lucky you found this out about Sheila. She's not in love with Pine and maybe she was never in love with you. She's a person who uses people and then spits them out. You are better off without her."

May straightened up and looked at Michaela, all traces of his previous drunkenness gone.

"You know, Mike, you're right. She's made me a fool, a fool for love. Wasn't there a song or a movie or something with that title?"

"If there wasn't, there should have been," said the bass player, who looked as though he had seen his share of ups and downs in the passion department. He bent down in front of May, his voice low.

"You gonna be able to do this thing with the cannons and all? You're the only one who's practiced it."

May stood up. "You bet I am. I owe it to all of you to pull it off." He gestured toward the orchestra whose members had gone back to tuning their instruments, the cacophony piercing the now darkening sky. "Those two aren't worth any more stress."

He nodded at Pine and Sheila, now in their places, pretending that nothing had happened. Michaela and the bass player did the same. I shook May's hand and walked back to the seat in the front row I had picked that was near where he would be coordinating the gunfire with the music. Luckily for all concerned, no one else had noticed the commotion.

For the next hour or so, the preparations continued by both the orchestra and the fireworks people, who I could see through my binoculars across the bay. The men around the guns on the opposite side of the bridge seemed to be finishing their work as well. Behind me, the chairs for the audience were filling up and so was the hill behind. There, parents with children and older couples were spreading blankets and setting up folding chairs on the grass. I could see Monk and Linda greeting people on the veranda of the headquarters building. Although I would have enjoyed sitting with them, I needed to be close to the action. I jotted down some notes until it got too dark to see them.

At 9:30, Monk walked to the front of the orchestra and tried out the microphone.

"Is this on? Can you hear me?"

Static and an ear-splitting, high-pitched screech came from all of the speakers around the area. A coastguardsman darted into view and turned some dials on a control panel to the left of the podium.

"Thanks, chief. The Coast Guard can't run without its chiefs."

A loud cheer rose from the back of the crowd. "Yeaaa, Chief Armstrong."

"On behalf of the United States Coast Guard, Yaquina Bay station, I want to welcome you to our annual Fourth of July celebration. I'm Monk Beasley, the commanding officer here."

Another cheer rose from the crowd. "Yeaaa, Mr. Beasley."

"I want to thank all of the businesses in Newport who helped make this event possible by donating food and drinks. I want to thank all of you for coming and for your support of our efforts here throughout the year. Tonight, as a special treat, I have asked the Oregon Coast Symphony Orchestra under the direction of Horatio Pine to perform for us. Without further delay, I present to you that orchestra. Maestro."

The crowd applauded as Pine walked out from the side, bowed to the audience, and turned to raise his baton.

Da da da dum.

And we were off, as the first fireworks bursts appeared in the sky. For its part, the audience's attention seemed divided between the musicians and the periodic blasts of flame. Beethoven's *Fifth Symphony* lasted about twenty minutes and when it was over, the audience applauded loudly and vigorously. The fireworks continued intermittently.

Next, Pine led the orchestra through George Gershwin's *Rhapsody in Blue*. Its many twists and turns and loud and soft parts proved to be an ideal accompaniment to the fireworks bursts. That piece lasted another twenty minutes.

It was now 10:40 and time for the big finish. As Pine took his bow and had the orchestra stand up to acknowledge the now deafening applause, I noticed Ted May standing up to the right of the stage, his headset on and the musical score in front of him illuminated by a tiny light on a music stand. His anger of earlier in the evening seemed to have faded, and his face was a picture of concentration as he contemplated the complicated synchronization of the artillery guns with the Tchaikovsky musical score. I had brought along a written guide to the piece, which I planned to incorporate into my article. I consulted it from time to time with the aid of a small flashlight.

The piece began as Michaela said it would with the cellos. She and the spiteful Sheila sounded wonderful as they began. It went on into a mixture of pastoral and militant themes, portraying the increasing distress of the Russian people at the hands of the invading French army with other instruments joining in. This section even included a Russian folk song.

In the real war, the turning point of the invasion occurred at the Battle of Borodino, where the Russian forces made their stand against what was up until then considered an invincible French army. Here the cannons would boom briefly over a few strains of *La Marseillaise*. As the fighting between Napoleon and the Russian forces intensified musically, it was time to cue the cannons again. This section was to be followed by a section of strings to depict the retreat of French forces. Next, victory bells and chimes would come in to show how the Russian people burned the city of Moscow to deny winter quarters to the invaders. Their subsequent retreat after as many as one hundred thousand casualties is not considered by historians to be a victory by either side. However, it did halt the French invasion and was the beginning of the end for Napoleon's plans to conquer Europe.

With the most spectacular of the fireworks dancing overhead, I could hear Ted May say "fire" as the orchestra played something like *da da da da-da, da da, dum dum dum*. The first volley of shells went off, landing in the water at the foot of the hill as expected. Something went wrong on the second burst, however. A shell struck the Yaquina Bay Bridge directly in the middle, causing part of the structure to collapse and sending a car into the bay. People in the crowd were alternately gasping in horror and screaming loudly at the sight, as the car plummeted end over end into the water far below.

The fireworks kept going off, as did a third volley from the artillery guns on the opposite shore. I turned toward the orchestra to see if Pine would stop the music. His eyes were closed, and he seemed oblivious to everything around him. Then I saw the figure of his lover, Sheila Cross, slumped over her music stand, her bleached blond hair touching the front of her dress. Even from this distance, I could see blood running down her lifeless face and dripping onto the floor of the makeshift stage.

PANDEMONIUM IS TOO MILD A WORD to describe the scene unfolding before me. Preoccupied with the horror on the bridge—the sound of the explosion and the sight of the car and its occupants plunging into the water of the bay—few people had noticed Sheila's slumped form on the stage. Amid screams and loud shouts, members of the audience ran to the rear of the grassy area and headed out the gates to safety.

Instinctively, I ran in the opposite direction and rushed toward the orchestra to see if Michaela had been injured—or killed. The bass player with the ponytail joined me as we removed the tangle of music stands and instruments left behind by the departing musicians.

Ted May was cradling his former wife in his arms and rocking back and forth. "Sheila, why did this happen? I loved you so much." He kept rocking back and forth and then began to moan softly.

Michaela was lying on her side several feet away from her chair. The guy with the ponytail—who I later learned was named Matt—was kneeling beside her.

"Is she okay?" I asked as I reached them, very out of breath.

The big man turned her over gently and began to give her mouth-to-mouth resuscitation.

"Mike, baby, come back to us," he said between breaths.

I stood and looked down at the prostrate form of someone I considered a good friend, although I had not known her very long. In a few seconds, she coughed and opened her eyes.

"Have I died and gone to heaven?" she asked, as she looked up at Matt. "You've never kissed me before." She started into one of her loud guffaws until she began to cough.

"Easy on the humor, Mike," he said, grimly. "Save it for the comedy club circuit."

He and I pulled her into a seated position, and she leaned against one of the chairs.

"Were you shot?" I asked.

She ran her hands up and down her torso and raised her blouse. "Under the circumstances, I won't ask you guys to turn your backs. Nope. Don't see any blood." She glanced around the chaotic scene. "What a nightmare. What happened?"

"One of the artillery shells hit the bridge at about the same time someone shot Sheila," said Matt.

"Sheila?" She looked perplexed and shook her head. "Is she dead?"

I looked over at Ted May still rocking back and forth and all the blood around him. "Looks like it."

At this point, Monk Beasley and two of his men ran over to us. All of them had their weapons drawn.

"Tom, is everyone okay? I scrambled my men as soon as the shell hit the bridge. We have had antiterrorist drills since 9/11, but it still took longer than it should have. I'm afraid I didn't pay any attention to all of you down here."

As he finished talking, he looked over at Sheila's body and the still moaning Ted May. He raised an eyebrow.

"That's his former wife, and I think she's dead," I said. "My friend Michaela Ross got knocked out but seems to be okay."

Monk talked into his cell phone.

"Ambulance is on the way." He glanced at Sheila. "I don't see how she could die from that shell hitting the bridge." He scratched his head in bewilderment and walked over to May. "Sir, could I ask you to lay your wife's head down and step away from her?"

May looked stunned, his eyes unseeing. He grabbed Sheila's body even more tightly, his rocking becoming more forceful.

"She's my wife." He shook his head. "I mean, she used to be my wife. She needs me."

"We will help her, if you'll let us." Monk's tone was gentle, but firm.

Still, May did not move.

"Maybe I can help." It was Matt, the bass player. He had walked over from Michaela's side. He leaned down and touched May on the shoulder. "It's okay, buddy. You've got to let these guys help Sheila. They are trained to help people in trouble."

May blinked and nodded, tears running down his face. "I know, I know. I've got to let her go."

He gave Sheila one last squeeze and then let her head touch the ground. Matt took him firmly by both arms, hoisted him up, and led him out of the way. Monk's men cleared the overturned chairs and music stands out of the area around the body. At that moment, I heard the shrill sound of an ambulance siren as it penetrated the still noisy and chaotic scene around us.

By this time, most of the people who had been sitting on the grass to hear the concert had fled so the vehicle had no trouble driving right up to where we were standing.

Monk walked over to the driver, and they talked for a moment. Monk pointed to us and shook his head. The driver and another attendant listened, then pulled a gurney out of the back of the ambulance and pushed it toward us. As they did so, Monk walked over to me.

"Tom, can I speak with you privately?"

We stepped away from the others.

"I told these guys that I think the woman is dead, but they said it would be better to get the body out of here right away to lessen the tension. I've got to coordinate the response to the bridge attack. I just wanted to see if you are okay."

"Thanks, Monk. I appreciate it. This had to be terrorism. But why here in Newport? It seems like a very unlikely target. I mean, we're so far off the beaten path."

"Yeah, I used to think that too. But somebody obviously had other ideas. I've got to go, but I'll keep you posted. If I were you, I'd get out of here and take your friend with you. This place is going to be crawling with *federales* in a few hours."

BEFORE I WENT TO BED THAT NIGHT, I worried that the night sweats and nightmares involving Maxine and Paul Bickford would come back. Until the events at the concert, I had decided that worries about my PTSD-like symptoms were over. Now, I wasn't so sure. Even after a long sleep, I still felt tired and shaky the next morning. If I had dreamed of my erstwhile friends, however, I couldn't remember.

After breakfast, I called Michaela Ross.

"Mike, it's Tom Martindale," I said to her voice mail. "I wondered how you are doing. Give me a call when you can."

I cleaned up the kitchen and went into my study. I sat down to look over the schedule of book signings my agent had prepared. As she had predicted, the publisher would not pay for any kind of national tour. They had agreed to reimburse my hotel and food costs in New York, Chicago, Denver, and Los Angeles. With all of the cutbacks and restructuring in the publishing industry, I felt lucky to get even that little amount of support. I had applied for, and received, a $5,000 travel grant from the university to defray those costs. I would fly to New York in a few days and spend a long weekend there, attending a few plays, visiting some museums, and participating in a book signing at the big Barnes & Noble store on Fifth Avenue. I hadn't decided if I would try to see Maxine. I called my agent but got only her message machine.

"Hi, Janet. Tom Martindale. I wanted to let you know that your plans for my book tour look good. I agree to all of it and will make my own travel plans. As per your agreement with Flatiron Press, they will defray my hotel and food costs, while I will pay for my own travel. I would appreciate it if you would fax me that in writing for my files. Please let me know about the bookstore visits when you have worked out the details. Thanks for all of your help. Also, I am hard at work on my articles for the collection and should have no trouble meeting the deadline. Bye for now. Call me when you can."

I hung up the phone and walked to the kitchen to pour another cup of coffee. The phone rang just as I was taking the first sip.

"Tom, it's Monk."

"Hi, Monk. How's your work with the *federales* going?"

"Tom, I've got some bad news for you. Your friend Ms. Ross has been taken into custody."

"Michaela? In custody? Where? The Lincoln County Jail? Can I see her? I might be able to help clear up whatever's involved. I was sitting near her."

"She's not being held by the sheriff, Tom. A federal judge signed off on an arrest warrant for her earlier this morning. She's been taken to a detention center in Portland."

"What kind of charge?"

"Violation of the Patriot Act."

FOR MOST OF MY ADULT LIFE, I have been known among friends as someone who tries to help people who I think need me. When I have done this, it has almost always been for altruistic, rather than selfish, reasons. I say "almost always" because I have to admit that I have, on a few occasions, had other motives in mind—like helping someone I care a lot about, such as a girlfriend. I did this many years ago for Susan Foster, a university biologist I was in love with at the time. I did it more recently with Maxine March—someone whose loss I still grieved. In both instances, I behaved honorably and really helped them out of their rather perilous predicaments—one a murder charge, the other a maniacal husband and his drug lord half brother. In both cases, however, I had gotten in way over my head and nearly been killed.

And yet, on this bright and clear summer morning, I hung up the phone and knew I was about to plunge into whatever tangled web my new friend Michaela Ross had gotten ensnared in. We were not lovers or even old acquaintances, but we had become good friends, and longevity has nothing to do with it when you know in your heart—and your gut—that someone was not being treated justly. Besides, looking at it somewhat

selfishly, her detention was a good story and one I had no intention of letting go.

I dialed a familiar number.

"Is he in?" I waited, then asked, "When will he be back from
court?" More waiting as the receptionist checked. "Please tell him
that I would like to see him right after lunch. Wait, does he usually eat at his desk? Good. Tell him Tom Martindale will bring him
some lunch at about one. Martindale. M-A-R-T . . . wait, make that
Tom Martin. He knows me. Great. *Muchas gracias*."

Given his predilection toward helping those who have been
treated unjustly and our earlier conversation about the infamous
Patriot Act, I knew Lorenzo Madrid was just the one to help
Michaela Ross.

✳ ✳ ✳ ✳ ✳

The waiting room was empty when I entered, but I knew the
way to Lorenzo's office in the back so I carried the bags of Chinese
takeout down the hall.

"I'm sorry, Tom, but I can't see you. I'm expecting a Tom
Martin."

Lorenzo smiled as he cleared a place on his desk for the cartons
of food. I lifted the white boxes out of the sacks, along with chop
sticks, plastic forks, and those tiny tubes containing hot sauce and
soy sauce.

"That is one of my many aliases. In my business, you can't
be too careful." I sat down and pushed some lemon chicken
toward him.

"And 'your business' would be what? Amateur sleuth of all
things academic?" He peered into the numerous containers and
held up his hand. "Let's eat before we get into your serious business." He expertly maneuvered a piece of chicken with a pair of
chopsticks. He handed me a pair.

"No thanks. I'll stick to a fork. If I used those things, you'd need to have your office repainted." I stuck the fork into a mass of beef lo mein, twisted it, and raised it to my mouth.

"Good."

"Don't talk with your mouth full, Tom." When Lorenzo smiled, he had a piece of fried rice hanging on the corner of his mouth. I pointed to it, and he whisked it away. We sat in silence for several minutes, enjoying the food and each other's company.

"Okay to talk now?" I asked, after another five minutes or so.

He nodded. "Be my guest."

"You know that I'm putting together a collection of my old articles, plus several new ones, including the one on you."

"Of course. I am going to be immortalized by you."

"Right. Count on it. Anyway, one of the other new subjects is Michaela Ross, a cellist with the Oregon Coast Symphony Orchestra. I met her recently, and she agreed to let me follow her around to rehearsals and concerts. I started doing that a few weeks ago, and last night I sat in the front row in Newport at the Fourth of July concert on the bay."

Lorenzo held up his hand. "Wait a minute! You were there when the shell hit the bridge?"

"I was."

"Holy shit. That's terrible, Tom. I had no idea. It was all over the news this morning, but I didn't have time to read any of the stories or watch TV very carefully. Anyone injured at the concert?"

"Not from the artillery shell. I guess the couple who were riding in the car that went off the Yaquina Bay Bridge drowned."

"You said 'not from the shell.' So someone died another way?"

"Yeah. Sheila Cross was a cellist too, and she was sitting right next to my friend. As the shell hit, she slumped in her seat. I saw it all."

"So what does that have to do with your friend . . ."

"Michaela Ross."

"Yeah, yeah, whatever."

"She is in federal custody under provisions of the Patriot Act."
Lorenzo dropped his chopsticks.

"If your friend was arrested for murdering this Sheila person,
there's got to be some mistake. The Patriot Act has nothing to do
with murder."

"That's why I came to see you."

＊ ＊ ＊ ＊ ＊

Lorenzo spent the next hour on the telephone calling various
people he thought might know something about Michaela. He
seemed to be getting nowhere.

"Whatever this is must be pretty big. I can't find out anything
from my usual sources. No one knows precisely where your friend
is or why she's there. You did say federal custody?"

"That's what my friend Monk Beasley of the Coast Guard told
me. And he's as federal as you can be, at least in the military part of
the government. Do you want me to call him?"

"Better not unless we need to. I don't want to compromise him. He
wouldn't be able to talk freely, and his phones might be monitored."

"You mean *tapped*?"

Lorenzo nodded. "You don't know the Bush Justice Department or you wouldn't ask that question." He thought for a
moment. "I've got one last possibility to try. I hate to do it, but
there's no choice." He began to punch in the number. "I'm calling
an old girlfriend who's an attorney with the Justice Department—
or would-be girlfriend, who had the hots for me until I told her I
swing the other way." He shook his head. "Took it hard. Thought
she could reform me."

He held up his hand.

"Erica? Hi, it's Lorenzo. I'm good. How are you? Great. Can you
talk for a moment? I need a favor."

I could hear her loud reply even though I was sitting across the desk. He held the phone away from his ear and waited.

"We both know I was a shit and behaved badly toward you. But I didn't lead you on. You have to admit that I did tell you the truth."

I felt embarrassed to hear all of Lorenzo's private stuff and got up to leave the room. He waved me back.

"You wanted something from me that was not possible for me to give you. I made that clear, but you wouldn't believe me."

More shouting emanated from the telephone.

"I am sorry, you know I am, but I want to make it up to you."

Lorenzo winked at me and smiled.

"Would you meet me for a drink tonight?"

He listened. The shouting stopped. Lorenzo was virtually cooing into the receiver.

"You know I never stopped caring for you, despite our . . ." he cleared his throat, ". . . differences."

He listened some more and wrote something on the pad in front of him. He smiled as he hung up the phone. "As the old saying goes, there is more than one way to skin a cat."

* * * * *

Lorenzo insisted that I drive with him to Portland, mostly because he thought I should not be alone after experiencing such traumatic events. He also suggested that, given my friendship with Michaela, I might be contacted by the FBI. "If you aren't home, they can't get to you just yet," he had said. While I waited for him to finish his afternoon appointments, he set me up in a small office down the hall from his.

It turned out to be the room that his investigator, Raymond Pearl, used. I sat down at the messy desk and looked around at the rogue's gallery of faces gazing at me from the walls. They all looked like Pearl—flinty-eyed, middle-aged men with weather-beaten faces and slicked-back hair. I would bet that most were former New York City police and Pearl's colleagues.

I killed time by again calling my agent to go over details of my upcoming book tour. This time she was in her office. I reconfirmed my plane and hotel reservations and even called the managers of the book stores where I would be speaking and signing books. Except for one—where the person who answered had never heard of me—they were all expecting me and had ordered my book.

At 6 p.m., Lorenzo stuck his head in the door.

"Ready to roll? I think we'll have missed most of the rush hour traffic by the time we get to Portland."

We walked to the parking lot next to his office building and got into his car—an older model Honda.

"Not very flashy for a big-time attorney," I said with a smirk.

"I'm supposed to be a servant of the people, not one of those white shoe, rainmaker guys at a big firm," he said.

"My car'll be safe here?"

"Yeah, don't worry. And if we get back too late, you can stay in my guest room and drive back to the coast in the morning."

We pulled onto Summer Street and then, after a few more turns, were driving north on Salem Parkway, then onto Interstate 5 to Portland.

"I'm meeting Erica in the Pearl District but only for drinks. She'll want to have dinner and something more intimate back at her loft after that, but it ain't gonna happen. I'll drop you at a restaurant a few blocks away and join you after an hour, and we can have dinner."

"That seems kind of cold," I said.

He shook his head. "You don't know Erica. When she sees that I haven't changed, she'll move on without batting an eye."

"But she'll have to try?"

"Precisely."

"I suppose timing will be everything—I mean, to get her to tell you what she knows about Michaela's case without playing a little hanky-panky with her?"

"That is why I'm such a skilled negotiator," he said with a wink. "I will be at my smoothest, although Erica will be tough. She's a real ball buster. I just don't want it to be my *cojones* that get busted."

* * * * *

First I had a drink, and then I ate a salad and a lot of sour dough bread at the high-priced, white tablecloth restaurant he dropped me off in the Pearl District. To kill time, I did all of this slowly. Much to my surprise, Lorenzo joined me in a little less than an hour.

"How are you and your *cojones*?" I asked him, smiling.

"Both intact, I am pleased to report." He slid into the booth across from me. "But after that, I need a drink."

As they always do in places like this, the waiter suddenly appeared. He smiled at Lorenzo, then blushed. "I'm Ty, and I'm your server. What can I get for you?"

Lorenzo flashed one of his biggest smiles, like the one that had discombobulated the women at the Italian place a few weeks ago.

"Hi, Ty. How's it going? Please give me a margarita, blended, with salt on the rim."

The waiter departed.

"Another conquest. You smile and the whole world waits with bated breath."

Lorenzo shook his head. "Everybody but Erica."

"She wouldn't tell you anything?"

"Not much, I'm afraid. This thing is big and the proverbial lid is on. The Bushies running the Justice Department don't leak very much. Erica is a career attorney out here on temporary assignment, so she is not as much in the loop as the *politicos*. But she does roll in the hay with enough of them to keep up to date." He munched some bread and took a sip of water.

"And? . . ."

Lorenzo looked around before he answered. "It seems as if the FBI has found a link between your friend Michaela Ross and whoever fired the shell at the Yaquina Bay Bridge. Because the bridge is a federal highway and a key transportation link, they are making it a national security issue."

"Michaela connected to terrorists? That's nuts. She's a symphony cellist, for God's sake."

"The problem for Ms. Ross is simple: she's all they've got, even though someone else fired the gun. I take your word for it, but you haven't known her very long. Could there be a link? You don't know, and I don't know, but the FBI found something incriminating—a fingerprint."

"On what? The cannon, the artillery shell?"

"Erica didn't know."

I shook my head. "This is bad, real bad. Will you help her?"

"Oh yeah. This is the kind of case I've been waiting for. There have been few legal challenges to the Patriot Act, and a lot of us have been waiting for a way to water it down. This might be a way to do that. I need to check into your friend's background more carefully before I go to bat for her though. She might be guilty as hell, and the whole thing could go up in flames. If we pick the wrong case, we'll lose the chance to win in court."

"Can you do this alone?"

"If I do it, I'll put together a team with a well-known person as the front man. I think I can get foundation funding for research and travel and expenses. I'm happy to do it pro bono because of the precedent it would set and the good a victory would do."

"You need someone to help with research?" I asked. "I've got time, and you hinted a few weeks ago at using me to do that."

"It just might work. Let's see what else I can find out. For now, I am going to be present at your friend's arraignment tomorrow. I'll get in to see her and offer my services first."

"Can I go with you?"

"She's being denied visitors except for an attorney. I want you to stay out of sight until we see if you are going to be dragged in."

At that point, Ty, the waiter, arrived with Lorenzo's drink. We ordered our food and ate it fairly quickly. When the waiter brought the check, he slid another piece of paper under Lorenzo's hand, who glanced at it and smiled at Ty.

"I am very flattered, but I'm way too old for you," he said in a low voice. The waiter looked dejected and walked away.

"These young guys think if they come on to you openly, you'll drop everything—especially your clothes—and run off with them," he sighed and shook his head, a sad look on his face. "It's not the way it works."

A pretty waitress brought the card and the paperwork back to the table for Lorenzo to sign. He signed it, and we left the restaurant quickly. We drove back to Salem without saying much—I think we both realized that what was ahead was daunting and a bit scary.

I decided to head home that night and arrived at my house after midnight. As soon as I walked in the door, I could sense that someone else had been there. I smelled sweet aftershave in the living room and found a cigarette butt in the kitchen sink. Everything else was as I had left it . . . until I reached my study. All of the drawers in my filing cabinets were open, and the stack of files I had left on the top of my desk was askew. On a hunch, I opened the one marked "Interview Notes" and discovered that the material on Michaela Ross was missing.

THE NIGHTMARES RETURNED THAT NIGHT. This time, I was standing naked in front of an orchestra, trying to both play a cello and use it to hide my private parts. Everyone in the audience and the orchestra seemed to be clothed, and they were, of course, laughing at me. They were waving what looked like sheets of paper from the reporter's notebooks I always used. As I tried to play, predictably only sour notes came forth, sounding like chalk on a blackboard. In the middle of all that racket, a single gunshot rang out. I woke up before I discovered the intended target. I wasn't sure if I had cried out, but I was sitting up in bed, sweating profusely. I squinted at the clock on the bedside table: 6 a.m.

As I lied back to calm down for a minute or two, I thought about the events of the day before. Michaela was in terrible trouble, but I was pleased that Lorenzo had agreed to help her. He had worked miracles for me a few years ago, and I was confident he could do the same for her.

BAM, BAM, BAM!

I jumped out of bed and walked quickly to the front door. I peeked out the small window in the door and saw a hard-looking face glaring back at me.

"Who is it? What do you want?"

"FBI. We have a warrant to search these premises!"

I cleared my throat to sound as authoritative as I could. "Hold some ID up to the window."

"Look, shit head, open this fuckin' door!"

"Let me see the ID first."

I was feeling more confident, I think because I was beginning to realize that some of these guys had probably been in my house the day before. But why had they returned?

"I'm waiting."

The same hard-faced guy held up his ID card. I opened the door and saw five agents wearing windbreakers standing around in a semicircle.

"Are you Mr. Thomas Martin . . ."

"M-A-R-T-I-N-D-A-L-E. Martindale. Yes, that's me."

"We have a warrant to search these premises."

He flashed some papers at me, but when I reached out to get them, he pulled them back.

"Don't I get to read the specific thing you are looking for, Agent . . ."

". . . Williams. This matter deals with a possible violation of the United States Patriot Act. We have been granted the right to seize your computer and any files we deem to be pertinent to our needs."

"Can I know the details of what this is about?"

"Don't answer that, Agent Williams." A short, wiry man stepped up to the doorway as the others parted to let him through. He was obviously in charge of this operation. I tried to cast off the uneasiness caused by my nightmare and this commotion and kept my voice steady.

"Tom Martindale." I held out my hand.

"Aren't you a cool one. Caleb Rutland."

We shook hands, and he handed me his card. He had the accent of a New Englander, possibly from Maine. His thin face made him a good choice to play the lead in a stage production of *Ethan Frome*, that old tale about people driven mad by the bleakness of their rural lives. I decided to test my observation.

"We don't find a Mainer on the Oregon coast all that often."

"You are observant, as well as unflappable," he replied with a half-hearted smile. "But we aren't here to discuss my place of birth, Mr. Martindale. We are here on serious government business. You will need to comply with this search warrant, or I will have to take you into custody as a material witness to a crime against the national security of this country."

I spread out my arms in a gesture of acquiescence and stepped aside. Rutland walked in, then stood to one side while the others entered and went through the motions of looking around the living room and kitchen, then disappeared down the hall and into my bedroom and office. For some reason, whoever had been here the night before had failed to find what they were looking for. I suppose they were trying to camouflage what they had done unlawfully then by returning in an official capacity today. Two of the men carried out a stack of my files. A third thrust what looked like a list into my hand.

"An inventory of what we're taking," said Rutland without turning around.

The remaining agents carried my computer out the door.

"I have to object to you taking my computer, Agent Rutland," I said. "I am a writer, and I need it to do my work."

He turned and walked over to me. "I am told that your local library has plenty of them for public use," he said coldly. "Try one of those." He turned to leave.

"I have to wonder why you guys didn't find what you were after when you broke in here last night for your little sneak and peek operation." The seizure of the computer had made me mad.

"Look, Martindale. Don't fuck with the FBI and, most of all, don't fuck with me. I'm not someone you want to fuck with."

Saying that, he walked out the door. Soon afterward, I heard the engines of two cars start. The tires squealed as the vehicles headed out of my driveway. My bravado disappeared as I sat down on the sofa. My heart was beating fast, and my head was beginning to ache as I contemplated what to do next. I showered and dressed quickly.

＊ ＊ ＊ ＊ ＊

"Lorenzo? It's Tom. I need you to call me soon, but use my cell."

I wasn't sure if cell phone calls could be traced, but I had had mine with me the day before so I knew that it had not been tapped. When he called back, I would take the phone outside. I walked out there now to make another call, in case my house was bugged.

"Hello. I'm trying to reach Paul Bickford. Is he there?"

I was expecting the soft drawl of his assistant whose name I had forgotten. This woman was more abrupt.

"And you are?"

"Tom Martindale. We're old friends and I just called to chat. We've been out of touch for a while."

"Mr. Martingale, I'm afraid that Major Bickford is not available."

"I'll bet he's on one of his secret missions to save the planet. Am I right?"

"Mr. Martingale, I do not think it wise for you to make light of the major's important work to protect our country."

This woman was all business, all the time, with no discernible sense of humor.

"Is that what he told you? What a kidder. He has not saved this planet or any other in the years I've know him."

"If there is nothing else, I have work to do, Mr. Martingale."

Saving a galaxy, no doubt.

"What's your name, in case I need to call again and ask for your help.

"Linda. Linda Lively."

"I'll bet you got kidded a lot in school."

"Good day, Mr. Martingale."

"Have a good one yourself, Ms. Lively."

I hung up the phone convinced that she definitely did not live up to her name now or at any time in her life.

I rummaged through an old address book and found another number. On a wild hunch, I dialed the number of Constantine Menzies, a photographer I had worked with who had been killed a year ago. He had given his photo business to my former lover, Maxine March. I assumed that the beneficence included his apartment in New York City. I stepped outside as I punched in the number. It was a beautiful day, and I took some deep breaths of air as I stood facing the sea.

"Menzies and March photo agency."

My heart skipped a beat when I heard her voice. I quickly disconnected. I felt foolish that I hadn't had the courage to at least say hello and ask about Bickford. He had been her contact when she was in witness protection, and I figured they had kept in touch.

"What a wimp," I muttered to myself.

Unless I ginned up my courage, I'd have to find another way to reach him. The phone trilled in my hand, and I jumped.

"Yeah, hello."

"Tom, it's Lorenzo."

"The FBI just served a search warrant on me and took my computer and some files. A nasty guy was in charge, an Agent Rutland."

"Tom, I want you to drive into town and find a public phone, then call me back." Lorenzo hung up.

Paranoia set in immediately as I stepped out the door. If Lorenzo was worrying about my cell phone being tapped, I might also worry that my house was being watched. As I got into my car and drove down the road, I kept glancing in my rearview mirror. When I pulled onto Highway 101 and headed south into town, I saw no suspicious vehicles on my tail. Like in the movies, I was looking for a dull-colored sedan with two men sporting bad haircuts. Only cars containing regular-looking people, pickup trucks pulling trailers, and RVs the size of buses were on the highway now, it being the peak of the tourist season.

Where to find an old-fashioned pay phone? They are rare in this era of cell phones and more sophisticated means of communication. I spied one in the lobby of the Lincoln County Courthouse where I had gone on a hunch that people who were on trial or their family members were less likely to afford cells—at least of the phone variety.

The first one had a line of three people waiting to use it. A tired-looking woman with two crying kids was first in line; next was a tall, thin man wearing a big cowboy hat and an earring in each ear. The third place was occupied by two teenage kids, male and female, with multiple tattoos and piercings everywhere on their bodies not covered with ragged clothing. They hung onto each other and giggled periodically.

I walked down the hall to an area away from the courtrooms and found what I was seeking. I dialed Lorenzo's number.

"Hi. This is your favorite client."

"Tom, excuse the melodrama, but I didn't want to take any chances that the feds had tapped your phone or bugged your house."

I told him more about Rutland and the suspicious entry of last night.

"They usually aren't that careless. If they did not straighten things up, they wanted you to know that someone had been there. As you say, Rutland probably wanted to make a show this morning to cover his tracks last night. It's sometimes hard to figure out how these guys think. I've heard of him since he's based here in the Salem office. He's tough and plays it by the book but sometimes breaks the rules and goes over the line when it comes to his tactics. Out here in the West, the FBI usually takes a laid-back approach. He's more old school. Comes from back East, I think."

"From the accent, I'd guess Maine," I said.

"Maybe he's trying to use this case to get back into the action," he said.

I told him about my trip to New York in a few days.

"Too bad you're leaving town," he said. "You could do some background research for me on this whole situation."

"Yeah, but I've really got to go. It's all set up. Maybe I can see Paul Bickford and get him to look into this. He's got contacts everywhere."

"He could be helpful," said Lorenzo. "At least the trip will get you out of Oregon. Rutland can't keep you from going on with your life. His warrant covered only your house, not you. If you aren't there, he can't mess with you. With a high-profile event like the bombing, I'm sure the town is crawling with federal agency cops and investigators from the Oregon State Police too. Best if you just disappear for a while. Leave a message on your machine that you will be gone for a week on a book-signing trip and will be back on a certain date. That way, it won't look like you've gone into hiding. Legally, you'd be clear and I'd back you up if anyone asks, which they probably won't."

"Should I leave your name and number as a point of contact—I mean, without saying you're my lawyer?"

"Good idea."

"I also like the fact that helping you with research would let me see this case from the inside—I could use that in my article on you."

"Why don't you stay with me until you leave town?" said Lorenzo.

"I don't have much space, but you're welcome to sleep in my guest room."

"Thanks. I'll see you late this afternoon then."

I drove back to my house—making sure that no cars followed me—packed a bag and my briefcase, emptied the refrigerator, and recorded the phone message. An hour and a half later, I was on my way to Salem.

ALTHOUGH I STAYED WITH LORENZO at his small house in Salem, I didn't see very much of him for several days. He worked very long hours and was usually up and gone before I got up. His house—a small, Craftsman-style bungalow built in the 1930s—was in an older neighborhood near the Oregon State Capitol Building. It was exquisitely furnished with expensive Mission-style pieces and Mexican paintings. On the wall of his bedroom was a striking photo of Lorenzo dressed in a white shirt and trousers like those worn by peasants. The white of the clothing made a strong contrast to his dark skin. When I asked him about it, he said only that it had been taken by his dead lover, Scott. Then he changed the subject.

I spent the days reading and looking up background on the Internet. On the second day of my stay, Lorenzo drove to Portland to attend Michaela's hearing, which had been postponed for several days. He had been allowed to see her only long enough to let her know that he was representing her. I could well imagine the stress she was feeling as she sat in a bleak cell in Portland without knowing why she was there.

"That's the horror of the Patriot Act," Lorenzo had explained.

"You can be held incommunicado for several days if the authorities decide to 'lose' you in the system. If I'm lucky today, I will find out more about the evidence they have, specifically the fingerprint."

I had wanted to go with him and at least wait in the hall, but Lorenzo felt I should not be publicly identified with her, given our plans for me to poke around the edges of the case.

Even though I trusted my agent to have done a good job with my speaking and book signing schedule, that afternoon I called all of the bookstores again—just in case she had forgotten something. I also double-checked my flights and hotel reservations.

After that, I worked on revising and updating the older articles that I was planning to put in the new collection.

Lorenzo phoned at about six to say that he had decided to stay in Portland because the hearing was going to extend into a second day. As per our previous agreement, I did not ask him any questions.

"Make yourself at home," he said. "I think there's plenty to eat."

After helping myself to a bottle of Mexican beer, I heated up a can of chili and warmed some tortillas to eat while I watched television. Then I read a while before going to bed.

＊ ＊ ＊ ＊ ＊

A report on the NPR station in Portland was the first thing I heard on the radio the next morning.

Sources in the federal courthouse say that a former member of the Oregon Symphony who now lives on the coast is being held as a person of interest in the July 4th bombing of the Yaquina Bay Bridge in Newport, in which a family of four died when their car plunged off the bridge at the same time as the annual fireworks display. Michaela Ross, 55, was playing her cello in a local orchestra when a stray artillery shell hit the bridge. Her fellow cellist, Sheila Cross, died of a single gunshot wound at that time.

Caleb Rutland, FBI agent in charge of the bureau's Salem office, said that Ross is being held under provisions of the Patriot Act.

—Jane Grant, OPB News

Even in my sleepy state, it was clear to me that Rutland was leaking just enough information to make it seem like Michaela was responsible for both the bridge bombing and the death of her fellow cellist. As if that vague linkage was not damning enough, he had also tied her to a violation of the Patriot Act. Since the attacks of 9/11, even the words "Patriot Act" brought to mind images of terrorism and disloyalty. Before long, anyone so branded was considered by all who heard their name to be a true enemy of the state.

I showered and dressed and decided to drive into town for breakfast. I picked up copies of both the Salem and Portland newspapers but found no mention of Michaela's arrest. Rutland had apparently orchestrated the leak so that it would first be heard on the radio. I was not certain of his strategy, but I was sure he had one. Even my limited acquaintance with him made it clear that he did not do anything without a reason.

A message from Lorenzo was waiting for me when I got back to the house. "Meet me at my office at one o'clock."

✳ ✳ ✳ ✳ ✳

Lorenzo had apparently canceled his appointments because his outer office was empty when I walked in. Even his secretary was not at her desk.

"Come on back," he shouted from the rear.

Lorenzo was dressed in one of his big-city power suits and looked like he could take on anything the federal government or a zealous FBI agent would throw at him.

"Sit down, Tom, and listen to an incredible story."

I accepted the cup of coffee he handed me and sat in one of the chairs in front of his desk. He loosened his tie and held up a file folder but did not hand it to me.

"This is what I was given by the feds, and it's pretty frightening."

"First, before we talk about that, how is Michaela? Does she need anything?"

"Sorry. I should have told you first off. She is doing remarkably well under the circumstances. She is one plucky lady. She is scared, of course. Who wouldn't be? But she says she is innocent and will work hard with me prove it."

"That's a relief. You said she *says* she is innocent. Does that mean you don't believe her?"

"No, no," he replied. "Just the contrary. I believe her and plan to help get her out of there as soon as possible and then to clear her name."

"I interrupted you—I mean about what they've got on her."

"Yeah. It's a convoluted story but plausible to some people in these scary times. You see, the Bush administration is always looking for would-be terrorists—foreign or American. Among their obsessions is the firm belief that there are sleeper agents all over the country waiting to strike when they can. Never mind that there have never been any such attacks by sleeper agents or anyone else since 9/11. But, against this background, a person like Michaela can be easily dragged into their net and ensnared there for a long time. On the surface, I have to say, it does not look good for her right now."

"No way is she a terrorist. That is ridiculous!"

"Hear me out before you dismiss the idea completely."

"You think that? If you do, maybe I'd better find her another lawyer who . . ."

"Don't get on your high horse, Tom. Just listen to me."

"Okay. Sorry."

"First of all, did you know that Michaela is of Lebanese descent?"

I thought back to my first interview with her. "Yeah, I guess she did say that her mother's family was from there. That's what they've got her on? Her ancestry? Wow, what a stretch!"

"As I mentioned before, the federal government has done something like this in the past. The Roosevelt administration used Executive Order 9066 after the Japanese attack on Pearl Harbor to round up one hundred and ten thousand American citizens along the West Coast in 1942 and move them into internment camps far inland, usually in bleak, desert-like locations. The order was upheld by the U.S. Supreme Court in 1944."

"I do know something about that. Some of my students' parents from eastern Oregon were subjected to that, and their families were rounded up."

"And these were American citizens, Tom! They had as much right as we do now to stay where they were. Instead, because of their ancestry and skin color and facial features, they were branded as traitors. It makes my blood boil even to think about it."

"Yeah, I feel the same way."

"The people in charge in this administration—I mean the people around the vice president, not the president, who is too dumb to be diabolical about anything—would happily do it again. Hell, if Latinos posed any kind of threat, we'd be on our way to camps somewhere too."

"So, Michaela's been arrested because her mother's parents came from Lebanon?" I said. "It's not even a Moslem country, is it?"

"Its government is divided between Moslems and Christians, but most people consider it an *Arab* country. Never mind that it has been the victim of terrorist attacks repeatedly over the years and has been used as a doormat for the more powerful countries around it. And, with its location next to Israel, it has long served as a training ground for all kinds of terrorists."

"Do they consider her a suspect in the killing of Sheila Cross?"

"Not so far," he said. "That killing seems not to be on the radar of the feds. I'd guess the state police and the local sheriff are investigating it."

"God, I'm glad Art Kutler's not in charge anymore," I said. "He'd already have me arrested, tried, and put on the nearest chain gang."

As I've said, Kutler, the local sheriff, had made a career of trying to implicate me in one crime or the other for years. I said *made*, past tense, because he had been shot and killed the year before in an incident at the Yaquina Head Lighthouse after it was disclosed that he had been taking bribes from the Mexican drug lord who has after me.

"Yeah, he was not your biggest fan," said Lorenzo, shaking his head.

He opened the file.

"I'll need to read a few things from this but not show it to you to protect Michaela's rights. She and I will use it in future deliberations about her."

He thumbed through a few pages.

"Okay, this is the main point of the charge: 'that Michaela Rashida Ross did knowingly consort with, and aid, a person or persons unknown, in a conspiracy against the United States of America and the state of Oregon by causing grievous damage to a property owned by both entities, to wit, the Yaquina Bay Bridge in Newport, Oregon. Because of her actions, said bridge—the roadway of which is U.S. Highway 101—was severed and a car bearing four occupants fell into the bay.'"

Lorenzo looked up at me and shook his head. "Quite a reach."

"Boy, I'll say. A true fairy tale. I don't see how any of this involves her. She was sitting in front of me and playing her cello when the shell hit the bridge."

"Here is the key part: 'Fingerprints of Michaela Rashida Ross were found on a shell casing next to the howitzer in the Oregon State Park by the Yaquina Bay Bridge where the errant shell was fired from during the annual Fourth of July fireworks display in Newport, Oregon.'"

I shook my head. "As I said before, how can she be in two places at once? She was playing her cello in a symphony orchestra, not putting hot rounds into a cannon several hundred yards away."

"Therein lies the mystery, and when we solve it, your friend will go free, and we will put a halt to this miscarriage of justice," said Lorenzo. "This is a textbook case of a zealous government trampling civil rights under the guise of protecting national security in a time of war, just like the suspension of habeas corpus during the Civil War or the unlawful imprisonment of Japanese Americans in World War II that we talked about before."

Lorenzo's eyes gleamed.

"I can't wait to get these turkeys into court. Notice the subtle use of her middle name—very Arabic—in the official charge. If that isn't prejudicial to a jury, I don't know what is. Michaela told me she had never used that name because she always wanted to be, as she put it, 'totally American'."

"So, what do we do? How can I help?"

"We talked yesterday about you doing research for me, and it was a bit vague. Now that we know all of this, you've got something tangible to work with. I'll explain what I mean in a moment. You have no trouble doing this?"

"Not a bit. I want to do it for her and because I also owe you. If this case succeeds, it will give your career a big boost."

He put up his hands and shook his head. "I'm not doing this to . . ."

"I know you well enough not to think that. You are serving the cause of justice—fulfilling the oath you took as a lawyer. Hell, let's be honest. I want to help Michaela, but I'm also doing this because it's a very good story that'll help me sell books."

"Okay, I think we've got our priorities out in the open. Let's talk about how we proceed. Want more coffee?"

"Yeah, my kidneys are floating but that discomfort helps me think."

Lorenzo laughed as he filled the mug.

"I did some thinking on the drive back from Portland, and I came up with a theory I think we'll go with for the time being. Obviously, Michaela was set up—by whom and for what reason we don't know. Why would a woman living on the western edge of the continent be someone a terrorist group would frame? How would they even know she is here or who she is? And the big question is, how did her fingerprint get on the shell casing?"

I shook my head. "Beats the hell out of me."

"Well, my friend, those are the questions you are going to answer. My investigator Ray Pearl is sick enough that he listened to me about retiring. That leaves an opening for you. He can still use his old contacts in law enforcement to help us; he just isn't well enough to travel. That's where you come in. Your trip to New York will provide the perfect cover. When are you leaving?"

"The day after tomorrow. What ties this whole thing to New York?"

Lorenzo smiled. "I thought you'd never ask. On a hunch, I asked Ray to call his old girlfriend who runs a car rental company in Lincoln City to see if anyone who did not fit the pattern of her usual customers had rented a car recently. She came up with a dark-skinned man—I'm being pretty judgmental, aren't I—from Portland who picked up a car on July 3rd and said he was going to be sight-seeing along the coast. He returned the car early on July 5th and said that his plans had changed. He even forfeited the amount he had paid for in advance. She was upset because the car reeked of cigarette smoke. She found a package of Turkish cigarettes shoved under the front seat. Another guilt by association thing on my part. See how easy it is? Anyway, Ray got his name and found out that he lives in New York—Queens, I think. The man flew back to Newark on that night's red-eye flight from Portland."

Lorenzo handed me an envelope.

"This is what I have on this guy. The name on his driver's license is Andy Hood. From the photo, it doesn't look like his name should be Andy Hood. Just like I'd never pass for a 'Knud Johanson.' This might be a bit dicey, Tom, so you need to be very careful. We can't get any help from the cops for now because that would tip off the FBI as to what you're doing. All these agencies share information, so they'd find out. I do have the name of a narcotics detective Ray used to work with, but he said not to call him unless you really get into a jam. He'd get in trouble for helping us get this ID stuff."

"Got it. His name's in here too?" I pointed to the envelope.

"Yes, it's there. What else do you need?"

"Nothing that I can think of. I'll make all of my arrangements tomorrow, then head up to Portland."

"Sounds like a plan. I've got some work to do on a few of my other cases this afternoon to clear the decks. Let's meet for dinner later."

Lorenzo and I had a great time that evening. We vowed not to talk about the terrorists or fingerprints or the Patriot Act—and we didn't.

He had left for work before I got up the next morning. I made some calls, repacked my bag, and was on my way to Portland by 1 p.m. I killed time at a movie theater before driving to the airport and catching the overnight flight on Continental to Newark.

JULY 10, 2007

I SLEPT FITFULLY ON THE FIVE-HOUR FLIGHT to the East Coast. As usual, Newark International Airport was a mess. Construction of one kind or the other had been going on there for years. The concourses and the baggage claim area were torn up, with temporary walls all but blocking passage. People had to lug their bags around barriers and questions to airport staff were met with shrugging shoulders and shaking heads. I made it through baggage claim and then outside to the area where shuttle buses to Manhattan loaded up.

At this early hour, fewer people than usual were milling around. I registered with the surly woman at the desk and walked outside to wait for the first van of the day. I liked the cheap prices and the no-nonsense approach of this company. The only problems came during rush hour when traffic delays and the need to drop everyone at their separate destinations made the fairly short ride take forever. Today, however, I was happily at my hotel—the Hotel Edison, in the theater district—in less than an hour. I left my bags with the bellman and walked over to Eighth Avenue for breakfast at a small luncheonette I knew about.

After I ate, I walked over to Broadway and then to the Rockefeller Center area. I have always enjoyed this time of day in the city. Proprietors were washing the sidewalks in front of their stores, delivery trucks were double-parked as drivers off-loaded boxes down chutes into basements, and people of all ages, shapes, and nationalities rushed by, most of them talking on cell phones or into the microphones of their Bluetooth devices.

Before long, a wave of dèjá vu swept over me. I was living here and starting my career in journalism and thinking, "I've made it! I'm working in the media center of the world. I'm working in New York."

※ ※ ※ ※ ※

After checking into the hotel, I grabbed a quick shower and changed clothes. I was eager to do what I always enjoyed about New York when I lived here: walking around town. For me, Manhattan has always been the most fascinating city in the country. Its mix of sights and sounds and unusual people is unmatched. You are always a block away from both opulence and poverty. And, you might see almost anyone or anything as you walk around.

My first stop this afternoon was the Majestic Theater to get tickets to a musical I had heard a lot about but never seen—*The Phantom of the Opera*. I have always been a sucker for big, splashy shows that are larger than life. Although the music might seen a bit plebeian—and the storyline a bit trite—to elitist reviewers, I loved it and played a CD of the score over and over in my car. Because of my interest, I happily paid the $100 for a seat in the mezzanine that night.

My next stop was the Barnes & Noble bookstore on Fifth Avenue. I had been there often as a customer when I lived here, but never as an author. I asked for the event coordinator.

"That would be Anna," said the young man with spiked hair, a pierced tongue, and five studs around the top of his left ear who was on duty at the information desk. "And you are? . . ."

"Tom Martindale," I said with some pride. "I'm the author scheduled to read and sign books here in the store tomorrow night."

The clerk yawned. "I don't think so." He pulled out a sheet of paper and consulted it. "Let's see. We've got a Martha Stewart/ Rachel Ray wannabe cookbook gal at 3, and then a guy who lived with Madonna for six months at 5."

He glanced at me. "What'd you say your name was?"

"Tom Martindale."

He squinted at the paper again. "There's a Tim Martin at 7. But that's not you—or is it?"

Just when you get carried away with your own success, a clueless guy like this can bring you down to Earth very quickly. I smiled weakly.

"Maybe it is. Is Anna here?"

"Oh, you want to talk to Anna? Why didn't you say so?" He picked up the phone and punched in some numbers. "Anna banana. It's Roland. Hi, dearie. Yeah, I'm at information. Yeah, the utter pits. So boooorrrring! Anyhoo—some guy out here wants to see you. Says he's an author, but he sure doesn't look like one!"

Roland winked and gave me a big smile. For the first time I noticed that he had some kind of sequins on his teeth.

"She'll be right down."

I walked away from the desk and checked out the section of true crime books nearby. I was happy to see a tall stack of my books at the front of the table. Next to it was a sign: *Author Signing, Friday Night at 7 p.m. See and hear Thomas Martindale, author of* The Cocaine Tale.

"Do you like the sign?"

I turned around to see a pretty young woman with a lot of hair and round, horn-rimmed glasses, which had slipped to the end of her nose.

"Anna Cushing," she said, offering her hand.

"Good to meet you. Tom Martindale. I appreciate the nice display."

She smiled.

"One problem, though. The title is wrong on the sign."

Her face fell. "Oh, poop! What's it supposed to be?"

"Like the book cover reads: *The Cocaine Trail,* not *Tale.*"

"Oh, double poop!"

She turned to Roland, still at his post at the information desk. "Roland, you asshole," she shouted. "You got the damned title wrong!"

He walked over to us. "Well, shit. So I did, so I did." As he smiled at me, one of the sequins fell from his tooth onto his lower lip. "I'll fix it—but not in your lifetime!"

Then he let out a cackle that was so loud a number of people browsing in the nearby literature and romance sections turned to look at us. I stepped back, as if to put distance between myself and this creepy guy.

"Just kidding," he said, after stifling a spasm of coughing. "I'll take the sign back to my trusty little workshop and make the change. Only the one word is wrong. Easy to fix."

He grabbed the sign, squinted at it closely, and walked away.

"Roland is farsighted but won't admit it," explained Anna, returning to her more dignified demeanor of before. "Let's go up the escalator to the area where you'll be speaking and signing."

We walked to the escalator and chatted as it took us up to the next floor.

"You on a national tour?"

"I guess you'd call it a modified one. I'm not that big a name to merit the star treatment some authors get."

"Yeah, I know what you mean. These publishers send the big-name people all over and spend lots of money on airfare and hotels and escorts and meals, but they don't need it to sell books. People will buy their stuff sight unseen. It makes no sense."

We reached the top of the escalator and stepped off.

"Over here, next to the coffee bar."

For a reason I have never understood, big chain stores always place their author event areas near the coffee bar so that authors must compete with the shouted orders for expensive coffee concoctions as they try to read a few selections from their books.

"How many people usually turn out for these events?"

"For big names, maybe fifty to a hundred. For you . . ."

"Not such a big name."

"I didn't mean to say that you weren't going to get people, I just meant . . ."

"No apology necessary, Anna. I know how this game is played. I'll be happy to read and sign for anyone who shows up."

As we shook hands and agreed to meet the following night at 6:30, I heard the familiar words "double macchiato with soy, extra shot."

JULY 11, 2007

IT WAS HARD TO KEEP MY MIND ON THE ANTICS of the Phantom that night, but I did enjoy the show. The next morning, I decided to take the subway to Queens to check out the address Ray Pearl had found for the guy who rented the car in Oregon. When I opened the envelope Lorenzo had given me, I discovered, among other items, a photocopy of an Oregon driver's license under the name of Andy Hood and a slip of paper with a Queens address. The dark-haired young man in the photo on the license had a heavy mustache and a two-day stubble and, as Lorenzo had said, did not look like he would be named Andy Hood.

Another photo showed Hood in front of some kind of military building, maybe an armory. He was with a group of men, all in U.S. Army uniforms, and someone had circled just him. A closer look revealed that he was clean-shaven and wore his hair cut close to his head. In this shot, he looked like he could be named Andy Hood.

There was also a copy of a police report from two years ago that described an incident in which Hood had been cited for blocking a driveway at the United Nations during an anti-Israeli demonstration.

I sat on the subway thinking about what I planned to do in Queens. In the first place, even going there was, to a New Yorker used to Manhattan, like going to a foreign country—a place you passed through on the way to and from Kennedy Airport. Although I had a map, I was not sure I could even find the address I was seeking. Manhattan is the easiest city in the world to navigate because it is, for the most part, very symmetrical. Queens, on the other hand, is a hodgepodge of streets laid out in no discernible pattern.

I got off the subway, which out here was above ground, and walked down to the street. Even with my map, I felt lost and in need of help. I raised my arm at a cabdriver who had slowed for a traffic light. He did a U-turn and pulled up in front of where I was standing. I got in, remembering how intimidated I used to be by cabbies. By the time I moved away from the city, I was barking destinations and suggesting routes like a lifelong New Yorker. But I was not as self-assured today.

"Where to, mon?" The black man had a lilt to his voice which suggested he was from the Caribbean, Jamaica maybe. That meant he would be more understanding to someone as lost as I was.

"Do you know how to find this place?"

He took the piece of paper from my hand and put on tiny wire-rimmed glasses to read it. "Let's see, mon, now I got my specs on." He smiled at me, gold teeth glimmering in the morning sun, and nodded. "I take you there. It not be far, my mon."

We drove five blocks, and he pulled over across the street from the address I had given him. He pointed to a building with a few businesses on the bottom floor and four stories above, presumably containing apartments.

"That be it, my mon."

I paid him and opened the door to get out. I hesitated, suddenly feeling very alone and vulnerable.

"How much to wait for me for one hour? I'm not sure if I'll be staying very long."

The driver stroked his perfectly groomed goatee and smiled. "I read my book and make an extra thirty bucks." He held up a copy of *Moby Dick*. "For my English class—literature to make me smart as you probably are."

"Great. Thank you. Just stay here, and I'll be back soon."

Luckily, one of the businesses on the ground floor was a small restaurant. When I entered—a bell on the door signaling my arrival— everyone in the place, including two children and a beautiful white cat, looked up and stared. As in many New York luncheonettes, this one was arranged with a long counter on one side and a series of small tables down the other.

I walked to one of the tables partway back and sat down as nonchalantly as I could, given all the stares. A middle-aged lady approached with a menu and a glass of water.

"We welcome you to Beirut in Queens."

"Thank you. I've heard a lot about your food." I usually stretch the truth when I need to. I handed the menu back to her.

"You no eat?" She was frowning.

"No, no. I want to eat. I just don't know what to order."

She pondered what I had said, as if to say, why would you come to eat food you have heard so much about when you don't know what it is?

"Okay, mister. I fix you good Lebanese breakfast you don't forget. Okay by you, mister?"

She smiled broadly, revealing even more gold teeth than the cabdriver had. The dentists in Queens had to have found their own mother lode somewhere nearby.

"Sounds good to me."

She returned quickly with a large, silver coffee pot and a small demitasse cup.

"Lebanese coffee is thick and strong," she said. "Also kind of sweet with spices and powered sugar. You drink with water."

I followed her instructions and took a sip, as she waited for my approval. It was good although a bit sweet for my taste, but I smacked my lips and motioned for her to pour more. I was on a roll with her, and there was no need to break this atmosphere of good feelings.

"You stick with me," she laughed. "I never steer you wrong."

As I waited for my food, I wished I had something to read. It is hard to remain nonchalant when you are staring at the table or at the walls or at the people sitting at the nearby counter and a table farther toward the back. Fortunately, the big white cat strolled by. I reached over to pet her. She let me stroke her fur for a few seconds and started to purr. Then, all of a sudden, she bit me and walked away. I cried out in pain and pulled my hand away. The whole place erupted in laughter. I joined the merriment, hoping my little feline friend had had her rabies shots.

The kind woman arrived with my food. "What I have for you, you will love, mister." She set two large plates in front of me, along with a basket of bread.

"Okay, mister. This is called *lubbneh* and has cream cheese, olives, and olive oil. This is *man'ousheh* and is a breakfast pie with all kinds of good things inside—meat, vegetables, you name it. And this bread is very tasty too. You enjoy, mister. I be back to make sure you enjoy."

I dug in, and it was all really good. I ate for at least fifteen minutes and barely made a dent in the large portions. Even though I would have no way to keep the food in my hotel room, I signaled the woman.

"You like my food?" she said, as she scurried over. "Is good, no?"

"Is good, yes. I loved every bite of it. Very good food. I am so glad I came in to your fine restaurant. Could I take some with me?"

"Of course, mister. I love to see my customers take food home. You live close by?"

"Ummm, uhhh. In Manhattan, across the bridge from Brooklyn."

"Oh good, mister. You tell your rich friends about this place? We serve breakfast, lunch, and dinner on weekends. Authentic Lebanese food like in the finest restaurants in Beirut. Ever been to Beirut, mister? It was often considered the Paris of the Middle East. Until all bombings and kidnaps."

She frowned.

"I get your bill and a box."

By this time, most of the people who had been inside had departed, presumably for work and school. Only the woman, the cat, and two men sitting at a table in the back remained. They had not turned around when I had walked in, so I did not see their faces clearly.

"Here you are," she said, putting the check in front of me.

I glanced at it. "This isn't enough. All of this for $10?"

"I give you discount so you bring your rich friends from Manhattan. We are open for breakfast and lunch and dinner on weekends. Okay?"

I guess I did have a look that was not common around this ethnic neighborhood. Even though I no longer lived in New York's most cosmopolitan borough, I was secretly pleased that I could still make that kind of impression. You never want to look like a tourist even when you are one.

"Okay, but I think you should charge me the full price." I pulled out my wallet and handed her a twenty. "I want to ask you about someone I am looking for, someone who might live upstairs. Do you know a man named Andy Hood?"

A look of fear briefly crossed her face, and she looked toward the men in the back. She shook her head slightly as if to warn me to avoid using that name again. One of them turned around and stared at me. He had the requisite heavy mustache and dark skin of many Middle Eastern men.

"No, mister. I just run my little place here. I don't want no trouble of any kind." Then she looked at the money. "I get your change."

"No need. The rest is for you. You took such good care of me. Thank you." I picked up the containers of food and walked to the front door. She and the cat followed me.

"Good day, mister."

She opened the door for me, stood aside, and then leaned in closer.

"I would not ask for this man in public," she whispered. "It could be dangerous for you."

Then with a wave of her hand, she said loudly, "Come again, mister. And bring your rich friends from Manhattan. We serve breakfast, lunch, and dinner on weekends."

I shook her hand and walked out into the street. I was relieved that the Jamaican cabby was waiting. He smiled at me.

"Glad you are still here," I said, getting into the back.

"I promised, mon. And you paid me the big gratuity. I am honest to a fault."

"I don't know your name."

"Call me Ishmael," he laughed, as he held up *Moby Dick*. "I think I like that name. Where do we go now, mon? Back to Manhattan?"

"Drive around the block and then park over there out of sight." I pointed to a side street and a place behind a delivery truck.

"Okay, I see we are going under the covers. I like the danger of that." He smiled, his gold teeth shining as he turned around and started the car. We were in place in a matter of minutes.

* * * * *

Ishmael returned to his book as I kept watch from the back seat. I hoped the men from the back of the restaurant would come out. But then what? Lead me to the guy I knew as Andy Hood? That would be too easy. And what if I found him? Did I seriously think I could confront him and get him to confess to blowing up a bridge on the other side of the country? In times like this—and there have, unfortunately, been many times like this in the past few years—I amaze myself at my audacity and stupidity.

After twenty minutes, I was ready to have the cabbie drive me back to the subway or even all the way into Manhattan, when the door of the café opened. The two guys stepped onto the sidewalk. One walked to the curb and held up his hand. In an instant, a long, black car pulled up, and he and the other man got in.

"Can you follow that car so the guys inside don't know they're being followed?"

"Trust me, mon," said Ishmael. "I love watching cop shows on TV."

Their car headed west on Atlantic Avenue, and we soon crossed into Brooklyn. We passed through the leafy luxury of Brooklyn Heights and into an industrial area near the on-ramp to the Brooklyn Bridge. The car ahead drove up to a large warehouse surrounded by a high fence with a locked gate. I had seen this area many times on my way into town from either La Guardia or JFK Airports.

Ishmael stopped the cab about a half-block back, and we watched the driver get out of the black car and use a key to unlock the gate. He drove through and then got out to close the gate and, presumably, relock it. The car disappeared behind the first warehouse.

I reached into my wallet and took out two fifty-dollar bills, which I handed to Ishmael.

"You dispensin' with me, mon?" he asked, looking a bit disappointed.

"Look, Ishmael, you've been a great help, but I think I will do better on foot now. This could get a bit dangerous, and I don't want you to get hurt."

"Why you do this, mon?" he asked. "You some kind of under the covers guy? This is serious stuff, mon. You could get zapped for good."

He seemed worried about me, and I was touched.

"It's a long story, and I don't have time to explain. I can take care of myself. I promise I won't take any chances. Just drive out of here and forget you ever saw me. Okay?"

Ishmael let out a breath of exasperation. "Okay, mon. Whatever you say. You are the boss, but I don't much like this scene. I can wait for you out of sight and just read my book."

I opened the back door and stepped out of the cab. "No, just get out of here. And thank you. It's been fun. Good luck with your education. That's the key to a good life." Mr. Professor offering yet another life lesson, as his goes into the abyss.

Ishmael started the car and turned it around in the narrow street. Without a glance in my direction, he drove away. Even before the car was out of sight, I regretted telling him to leave.

I walked up to the gate and, as I expected, found it securely locked. I walked south along the high fence hoping to find some kind of opening—an unlocked gate, a hole, a rusty fence post. Nothing.

Just as I was ready to give up, I saw a black cat emerge from an opening in the fence a few yards away. I walked quickly to that spot and discovered a gap where a section of the chain link had rusted, leaving an opening the size of a small window. I eyed it carefully and hoped I would not tear my clothes or become entangled in the jagged prongs as I tried to slip through.

Careful now, I muttered. Just take it easy, and you will . . . Shit. My belt was caught. I moved back and dislodged it so I could try again.

"Why you follow us?"

From my low vantage point, I saw only the polished shoes of one of the men as I managed to move to the other side of the fence. I stood up.

"It's my cat. I lost him. Silly guy. He ran away from me after he got out of his carrier. I was taking him to a friend who was going to watch him. . . ." I could blather with the best of them.

"Stop," said another voice. "Do not insult our intelligence!"

A man I hadn't seen before walked up to the fence, as I began to back away.

"Are you FBI? CIA?" He looked genuinely puzzled.

I kept moving backward. "Nothing like that." I raised my hands and shrugged my shoulders. "Me? I'm just a guy who lost his cat."

Just then the bedraggled feline who had inadvertently showed me this opening walked up and bared his teeth.

"There you are, Blackie," I cooed. "What a naughty cat you are. Come to Papa."

The cat hissed and tried to bite my leg. I knew then why I had always preferred dogs: they idolize you and constantly let you know that you are the boss.

I started running across the street and darted behind another abandoned building. The men yelled in Arabic and ran along the fence, presumably to get to the car.

I ran as fast as I could for about three blocks but was soon so winded I could barely breathe. As I fell to my knees, I heard a car pull to a stop behind me. I braced for a beating or a bullet.

"I told you, mon. You should not have gone into that place all alone."

IF THE MEN IN THE BLACK CAR HAD TRIED TO FOLLOW US
back to Manhattan, Ishmael lost them through a series of evasive
maneuvers worthy of a stunt car driver. We crossed the Brooklyn
Bridge and then sped along back streets around city hall and
Chinatown to the West Side Highway. Then he drove north to the
theater district where he let me out on Eighth Avenue and 50th
Street, a few blocks away from the Hotel Edison just in case the men
were still following me at a distance.

"How can I thank you, Ishmael?"

"Just hold a good thought for me for success with my schoolin',
mon."

I grasped his hand tightly and gave him another fifty-dollar bill.
"I will do that."

I waved as he pulled away from the curb and into the heavy flow
of traffic on Eighth Avenue—an unusual gesture for New Yorkers
who often exit cabs cursing and bemoaning the rude way they had
been treated and cheated. Within ten minutes, I was in my room
and in the shower, hoping the hot water would calm my nerves.

* * * * *

When I emerged from the hotel two hours later, I scanned the street in both directions before walking east toward Broadway. The dark car and dark men were nowhere in sight. I needed to clear my head and walk off that heavy Lebanese breakfast. I walked to Rockefeller Center and then over to Madison Avenue. After ten blocks, I headed across town on 66th Street—past the tall edifices of Park Avenue, where some of the richest people in the United States live, and into the mixed commercial and residential neighborhood along Lexington Avenue. I had lived in this area in the 1970s and early 1980s before I moved to Oregon to start my teaching career at Oregon University.

It was a bustling area along Lexington, a major north-south thoroughfare, in contrast to the landscaped side streets where some of the most expensive townhouses in the city were occupied by an elite group of people who sent servants to shop in the neighborhood where I had lived.

I walked down 66th Street alongside the big armory that extends from Park Avenue to Lexington, then I crossed Lexington and stood in front of the magnificent St. Vincent Ferrer Catholic Church. The building I was looking for was straight across from here. I looked at the small piece of paper in my hand to verify the address. Yeah, 882. That was where Constantine Menzies had lived and where I figured Maxine March was now living.

I walked into the church and sat for a moment to rest my legs and contemplate what I would do next. The peace and quiet of the sanctuary helped calm the stress I was feeling after my morning of danger and escape and evasion.

Beyond doing the book signing that had been my pretext for making the trip, I had two goals while I was in New York: to find out who Andy Hood was and what his connection was to Michaela Ross and to try to see Maxine. I got up and walked out the main door. I knew I couldn't stay here for very long, given the vigilante-like view many people had of strangers in the post-9/11 world.

I pretended to consult a guidebook as I went down the stairs and turned to the left, but I was really looking across the street at the windows of the front apartment on the top floor: #4-A. On my second or third glance, I noted that a woman was raising the blind.

My heart stopped. It was Maxine, and she was looking out as if checking the weather for the first time that day. She must have slept late or been working inside on some photos. She turned to face a man who walked up behind her and put his arms around her waist. She kissed him, and they both turned to look out the window.

I froze. *Paul Bickford.* A friend I had depended on and trusted for years had betrayed me.

Logic was not playing any role whatsoever in the fury I now felt. I hailed a cab and returned to the hotel as fast as it would take me. By mutual agreement, Maxine and I had broken up the year before. The problems in our relationship—caused largely by my own jealousy and stubbornness—were insurmountable. We both knew that and accepted it. She had moved on to a new life, one largely provided for her—not by me but by Paul Bickford. He had set her up in the Witness Protection Program and had been the only person to know where she was. Now, he had eased his way into her new life in New York.

But still. . . . He and I were good friends who had been in our share of narrow escapes together, and I did not feel that a good friend would start sleeping with the other's lover. I shook my head at the memory of what I had just seen, as the streets and people on the sidewalk rushed past the windows of the speeding cab on its way downtown. The fact remained, however, that I needed him now to find out what the FBI had on Michaela and who Andy Hood really was. Without Bickford, my investigation was stalled.

Later, in my room, I decided to swallow my anger and try to get him on the phone. I dialed a number and waited while it rang.

"Menzies and March photo agency."

My voice would not emerge from my throat.

"Hello?" She seemed to turn her head to speak to someone in the room with her. "I can hear someone on the line, but they won't say anything."

She said into the phone, "Do you need a photographer?"

"Maxine?" My voice croaked as I said the word.

"Yes." She sounded hesitant, as if she recognized a voice from the past but was not entirely sure if she was right.

"Maxine, it's Tom. How are you?"

"Tom. What a surprise. Where are you?"

"I'm in New York, for a book signing."

"I read about your book. Seems like it's making quite a stir. Congratulations. I know how hard you work on your books."

"Yeah, well, it's always a hassle. Not sure why I do it. I guess I'm a masochist at heart."

"I wish you well, Tom. I think you know that. I hate to be blunt, but why did you call? You know, I don't think it would be wise for us to get together. We've both moved on—at least, I've moved on."

"And I am not capable of moving on?" I regretted the sarcastic words the minute I uttered them.

"You will never change, Tom Martindale. I've got to go. I've got work to do."

"Wait. I'm sorry. You know I'm always sorry after these out-bursts. I'm a jealous guy, I know that. You know that."

"Tom, I am not your analyst. I'm going to hang up now."

"Wait. Is Paul Bickford there?"

"Paul? Why would you think he's here?"

Letting her know that I saw him in the window with her an hour ago was, of course, out of the question. So I lied.

"I tried to call his office, and they said I might find him at this number." I closed my eyes and crossed my fingers that she believed me.

She hesitated, as if looking at Paul for permission to reveal his presence there.

"Tom, you dumb son of a bitch," said Bickford, after grabbing the phone. "I know my assistant would never tell anyone where I was. Are you following Maxine or spying on this apartment?"

I could hear him walking on the wood floor of her apartment, probably to look out the window onto Lexington. The blinds rattled and he resumed talking.

"Are you out there, hiding in the church maybe?"

"Nice to talk to you too, Paul. It's been far too long. No, I'm in New York but down in the theater district. I knew you helped Maxine get set up, so I took a chance that she might know where you were. Your assistant would not give me the time of day, but I need to see you. I need some information that only you can get for me."

"Don't tell me. You're involved in one of your harebrained investigations. And it somehow involves the United States government. Shit! When will you learn to keep your damned nose out of this kind of thing? And what makes you think I want to get involved with anything you're associated with? My promotion was delayed for a year the last time I saved your sorry ass."

"I know, I know. All you say is true. And yet . . ."

"Where are you and when can we meet? For reasons I have never understood, I am never able to ignore you."

BICKFORD HAD ALWAYS BEEN ABLE TO ADAPT to whatever surroundings he was working in. From the Arctic to the Oregon coast to Manhattan, he looked the part, no matter what that "part" had to be. As he walked toward me in the slightly shabby lobby of the Hotel Edison, he could well have been an executive in a large company, not one of those most skilled operatives in the U.S. Army clandestine service. His navy blue, patterned tie perfectly matched his pinstriped suit of the same color. The cuffs on his white shirt protruded equidistant beyond the sleeves of his coat.

"Good God, are those cuff links I see?" I said, as we shook hands.

"You bet your academic ass," he said, smiling. "Golden eagles with pieces of flesh in their talons."

"I know the feeling after hanging around with you from time to time." I glanced around. "Where do you want to go?"

"This place doesn't feel right. Follow me."

We walked out the door, and he hailed a cab. We got in, and he gave instructions to the driver, a man of indefinite nationality who was wearing a turban. The cab pulled away from the curb, and we were soon heading across town at a high rate of speed. We both looked out our respective windows, willing to wait until we reached our destination to talk. Ten minutes later we were there. I got out first and let Bickford pay the cabby.

"Ever been to Paley Park before, Tom?"

"Yes, many times when I lived here."

We walked into one of New York City's first so-called "vest pocket" parks, a pleasant oasis from the maddening crowds trudging by outside its iron gates. The former president of CBS had paid for the construction of the small gem, which had trees and planters and a wall of cascading water in the back. Visitors could buy coffee and snacks and sit on chairs to rest and read their daily newspapers.

Bickford stopped at the food kiosk. "You take your coffee black, if my memory serves."

I nodded and walked over to a table next to a side wall near the back.

He soon joined me.

"Good. You picked a place where the water will drown out what we say."

"I have always thought you were paranoid but in this case, I'm thinking you are right."

"I've created a monster," he laughed, taking a sip of coffee. He made a face.

"Not the best I've ever tasted." I drank from my cup and nodded my agreement.

"Okay, Tom. Let's have it. What is this all about?"

It took me about ten minutes to fill him in on the bombing, Michaela's arrest, Lorenzo Madrid's defense of her, and the possible involvement of the Lebanese man called Andy Hood.

"It goes without saying that you should not get involved in any of this," he said, when I paused to drink more of the foul-tasting coffee.

"I saved the best until last. I was visited in my house by FBI agents from the Salem office, led by a Caleb Rutland."

I shoved his card across the table. Bickford picked it up.

"Mind if I keep this, Tom? I'll make some inquiries. Did he say anything about you being under suspicion and not leaving the state?"

"No, he just questioned me about how I knew Michaela and took my computer hard drive and some files. I had the feeling, though, that he's the type of person who would just as soon throw you in the clink as look at you."

"And he might be looking for you by now."

"But I didn't have anything to do with firing the artillery shell at the bridge."

"From what you say, neither did your friend Michaela Ross."

I nodded.

"But you've always been trying to help one friend or the other ever since I've known you."

"And one friend in particular is now a special friend of yours."

Bickford held up his hand. "Let's not go there, because I don't think you are capable of thinking rationally where that 'special friend,' as you call her, is concerned. If you make this about the two of you or the three of us, I'm going to get up from this table and walk away from you and this latest problem of yours."

I raised both hands, palms open, in that universal sign of surrender.

"Sorry," I said. "Like you say, I'm not very rational when it comes to Maxine."

"Agreed—and enough said. She is happy in her new life and busy in her career, and let's just leave it at that."

I nodded and sipped more of the, by now, cold coffee.

"Let me tell you a little more about the Patriot Act," he said, after looking again at Rutland's business card. "People in all federal agencies involved with national security have to consider it the Holy Grail—that is, if they ever want to be promoted or avoid being reassigned to some backwater office in the boondocks. That act has many faults and was passed too hastily in the burst of anger and patriotism following the 9/11 attacks, but it is now the law of the land, as we say."

"Boy, you can say that again. The Bushies really rammed it down the throat of Congress in those early days. I'm no expert on it, but it seems to me that an awful lot of our civil rights were taken away in the name of national security."

"And no one blinked," he said.

Bickford glanced around the tiny park, probably trying to make sure that everyone present belonged there at this time of day. A Hispanic nanny with two small, blond children in one of those expensive double-wide strollers. A young man and woman holding hands and gazing into each other's eyes. An older woman reading *The New York Times*. A middle-aged man in a New York Yankees cap and matching sweatshirt working a crossword puzzle. A girl in an all-black Goth outfit, with multiple ear and nose piercings and purple hair.

"Look, Tom, you know I've never been a political person. You can't afford to be when you're in the military. My job is to listen to whatever order I'm given, salute, and carry it out. I've always done that and, I like to think, done it well. But I have grown to hate the Patriot Act because some of the people who are being detained are being deprived of due process. Habeas corpus is out the window. It seems like your friend is a victim of that. I don't like it. I will try to help you as much as I can because of my distaste for that particular law. But I can only give you information. I can't get directly involved. My ass would be in a sling very fast if anyone above me in the army or any federal agency thought I was doing anything to interfere with an investigation by the FBI. We will have to be very careful, even talking on the phone. And I don't think we should meet again for a while."

He looked around to double-check the people in the park. An older couple had appeared, both carrying shopping bags, probably holding their purchases after a foray into the shops on nearby Fifth Avenue. They seemed safe to me, and Bickford seemed to agree because he relaxed a bit. At this point, I decided not to say anything more about my trip to Queens to find Andy Hood. It was better to handle one thing at a time.

"Let me make some calls and see what I can find out. It won't be pleasant for either of you, but I think we should use Maxine as our go-between. I'll let her know where I am and what to tell you when you call. I doubt her phone is tapped. Use this new cell phone when you call her. It's one of mine and can't be traced."

"Thank you, Paul. As always, I appreciate your help. I know I shouldn't keep dragging you into my stuff, but . . ."

He raised his hand.

At that moment, one of the men who had seen me in the Lebanese restaurant in Queens walked up to the table and sat down.

Bickford looked perplexed but before either of us could say anything, the man pulled out a knife and lunged at my throat. As I pulled back, Bickford shot him in the chest. Without a sound, either from Paul's gun or the man, he slumped in his chair.

Bickford motioned for me to get up, and we walked slowly out of Paley Park as the other people continued enjoying their respite from the dizzying whirl of daily events, oblivious to what had happened in this pleasant park in one of the busiest parts of one of the busiest cities in the world.

"I GUESS YOU PLANNED TO FILL ME IN LATER about a man in dark glasses who might be looking for you," Bickford whispered, an edge to his voice.

I started to answer, but he cut me off. "I'll be in touch."

We walked swiftly out onto East 53rd Street together, then he headed toward Madison Avenue and I walked to Fifth. I expected someone—the police or another bad guy—to run after me, but no one did. Strange as it seems, the whole incident had happened without raising the suspicion of anyone sitting near us in the tiny park. Before long, someone would see the dead man in their midst and scream and call the police. By then we would be gone.

I crossed Fifth Avenue and walked into Rockefeller Center. I headed for the area that was a skating rink in the winter but was now a large outdoor café. I walked around acting as if I was waiting to meet someone, but I was really paying more attention to the crowd, especially guys in police uniforms or dark men in dark suits.

When I was safely back in my hotel room, I quickly packed my suitcase and called to check the status of my flight to Portland that night. I had decided to go through with the book signing, then leave for Portland.

* * * * *

I walked into the Barnes & Noble bookstore on Fifth Avenue at
6:30 p.m., a half-hour before my signing. The same bored clerk with
the studs around his ear and sequins in his teeth was on duty.

"Good evening, Roland."

He looked up from a book by Nietzsche that he was reading
intently. "How do you know my name?"

"I am very quick. In addition to the name tag there on your
shirt, I was in here yesterday, and you introduced me to Anna."

"Oh, yeah. You're that Tim Martin guy who wrote a book on
marijuana."

"Wrong name but close on the drug. Tom Martindale and the
book is about cocaine."

"Oh, shit. Yeah. *The Cocaine Tale.*"

"It's *Trail*. Like the Santa Fe Trail."

"Huh?"

"People rode along it to get to the West in the nineteenth
century."

"Did they carry drugs then too?"

He was seriously deficient in both his knowledge of American
history and his general level of intelligence, except maybe for knowing a little bit about Nietzsche.

"Never mind. Is Anna here?"

He reached for a phone and punched in some numbers.

"Anna banana. It's Roland. Hi, dearie. Yeah, I'm back in information. A serious waste of my knowledge of literature, but what can
I say. It's a job. That guy from yesterday is back again. Mr. Cocaine."

He smiled at me as he listened to her reply on the phone. He
rolled up a dollar bill and pretended to snort something up his
nose. He pointed at his nose and nodded. I quickly shook my head
as he pressed the OFF button and put the phone down on the desk.

"She'll be right down."

He returned to his book and did not glance at me again.

The perky Ms. Cushing was soon at my side.

"Welcome to Barnes & Noble, Mr. Martindale. Or is it *Professor* Martindale?"

Roland looked up in feigned horror. "You're a professor? God, had I known a member of the Grammar Police was here, I would have watched what I said. Was I grammatically correct at all times?"

Before I could answer, Roland burst into one of his loud cackles, again causing people in the nearby literature and romance sections to turn and stare at all three of us.

Anna ignored him and led me gently by the arm to the escalator. "As I told you yesterday, we hold our signings and readings up on the mezzanine, a bit away from the crowds on the main floor."

The conveyance lifted us quickly to our destination, and we stepped off.

"This way, Professor M," she said smiling.

My new name, but I liked it. Anna was young enough to be one of my students, and I related to her easily.

"Here we are." She pointed to the area I had seen before where a podium had been set up facing two rows of ten chairs each. I wished my back could be against a wall, but instead it was in front of the coffee area.

"Do you need any visual aids?"

"No, just a mike."

She walked to the podium and pulled out a wireless microphone.

"This should work for you. Just flick this little switch on the side, and you're in business. I'll be introducing you, so it will already be on when you start to speak."

She handed me the mike, and I glanced at it before giving it back to her. Even a technophobe like me should be able to handle this.

"The table for your signing is over here." She pointed to a table containing four stacks of books, maybe ten per stack. "There are more below if we need them."

"Anna, if I sell even half of those on the table, I will be ecstatic."

"That should be no problem. This is New York City, the capital of book publishing and a mecca for readers."

"Yeah, I guess you're right."

People were beginning to fill up the seats.

"See, I told you so," said Anna. "I'm going to go back to my office and get your bio stuff."

I walked over to two of the people who had sat down—a distinguished-looking couple in their sixties.

"Tom Martindale. Thank you for coming."

He shook my hand and she smiled.

"Dag and Kathleen Kremer. Our son became addicted to cocaine during his first year in college. I am happy to say that his rehab has been a success. I'm a doctor and my wife is a nurse, so we've seen firsthand the effects of drug abuse all of our professional lives. We'd like to know how this stuff gets into the country."

"I'm glad he is doing well," I said. "I hope the information helps you understand the situation better."

Another guy with spiked hair and lots of piercings and tattoos was sitting behind the Kremers.

"Handler," he said, giving me a weak handshake. "One name only. I prefer weed myself, but I thought I'd find out about other drugs I may want to try." He smirked and the Kremers both turned around and glared at him. "I'm just askin'," he said. "Not sayin' I'm usin'."

I walked back to the podium, and Anna joined me there. About ten more people had sat down in the chairs. I would not have to feel embarrassed about the turnout.

"We'll wait a few more minutes to let the seats fill up," she said.

Over my shoulder I could hear the shouts of the workers as they placed the coffee orders with the barristas. "Double shot of espresso with skim. Macchiato, extra hot with room for cream. Cappuccino with no foam." And so on until Anna took the mike.

"Good evening, everyone. I want to welcome you to the latest in a series of books in the news, designed to bring to your attention works about subjects that are important to all of us. I'm Anna Cushing, the assistant public events manager here at this Barnes & Noble store. We at Barnes & Noble feel that it is vitally important to keep our readers informed about events and issues that shape their daily lives."

I glanced around the area as she paused and was surprised to see Paul Bickford sitting in the back row. Next to him, looking a bit apprehensive, was Maxine March. As always, my heart skipped a beat as our eyes met. She looked away quickly, breaking the spell, and took hold of Bickford's hand. If ever there was a sign of my dismissal, that was it. I looked down at my notes. Anna finished introducing me, and I stepped forward to a smattering of applause.

"Thank you, Anna. It is my honor to be a part of this Barnes & Noble series on books in the news. Drugs have ravaged this country for many decades. Drug use is up in every state, and more and more people, especially the young, are ruining their lives by taking substances that will lead to addiction and death."

I glanced at the young man called Handler and at the Kremers as I said this. I continued to speak about drug use in general and then brought the audience to my particular story in Oregon—of my accidental involvement with a Mexican drug gang, of the effect this had on my life and those I cared about, like Maxine. Although I did not use her name or identify her now, I did look at her from time to time.

As I was beginning to read a selection from the book, a young man walked up to me from behind, interrupting me.

"Could you keep it down," he said. "Some of us are trying to study over there." He pointed to the coffee area.

Anna quickly stepped up and took him by the arm. She was talking in a loud whisper as she led him away.

"That was a nice way to bring my level of self-importance under control."

The audience laughed.

"Very rude," said a voice.

"Hire the teenagers while they still know everything," said another to more laughter.

"I always worry that I am boring my audiences, so let me cut it short here and answer any questions."

Handler was first on his feet, but I ignored him to field queries about my methodology of fact-gathering and whether I found it hard to write about myself and those I know. That was followed by the usual questions about getting an agent ("Hard to do but important") and my thoughts on the state of publishing today ("Dismal with self-publishing, a once reviled part of the business, but becoming more widely accepted").

Handler kept raising his hand, so I finally called on him.

"Yes, sir."

"The woman you refer to as 'M'—is she a real person or a composite?"

Maxine winced and again squeezed Bickford's hand. This was the same phrasing used by the young woman at the book signing in Portland. I was beginning to smell the proverbial rat.

"She is a real person who I felt I had to protect in the book because she was a key witness in the government's case against the drug dealers."

"Isn't it true that you were romantically linked with her in the past and stepped into her life after her husband was killed?"

Handler had to be from the same online blog as the woman in Portland.

"Who are you with?" I asked him.

"Oh, sure, man, sorry I didn't say. I'm with the Under-the-Cover Dot Com blog. We give our readers an inside look at the publishing world."

I looked again at Maxine, who was near tears. I could not—no, *would* not—identify her now. For one thing, it would serve no purpose. For another, it would add to her hatred of me.

"I think I'll just dodge that question and hide behind the old cliché about it all being in my book, which I will be happy to sign for you now."

As Anna led me to the table, I saw Maxine rushing to the escalator, Bickford close behind. As he departed, he made a point of holding up his cell phone and mouthing "call me." I nodded and turned to face my eager fans, pen in hand. I signed twenty books over the next half-hour—a very respectable showing for an unknown author from the Pacific Northwest appearing in New York City for the first time.

USING THE CELL PHONE HE HAD GIVEN ME, I called Paul as soon as I got back to the hotel. I hated to risk having to talk to Maxine again, but hers was the only number I had for him. Even though I had thought about her constantly in the months since I last saw her, it was depressing to talk to her.

But finding out that she and Paul were seeing each another—maybe even living together when he was in New York—spoke volumes about the status of our relationship. It was over. I could get angry and yell and cause a scene. But I could also face the inevitable. Maxine and I no longer had any kind of future together. Hell, we probably weren't even friends.

Bickford picked up after one ring.

"Paul, it's Tom."

"I figured. Glad you called me quickly. Have you talked to your lawyer?"

"No, I planned to call him as soon as I talked to you. I've been concentrating on my book tour."

"And your investigation of would-be terrorists?"

"There is that, yes."

Bickford constantly razzed me about my tendency to get involved in things I should avoid.

"You better call him fast. You need to get back to Oregon. You are in some trouble."

"How so?"

"That FBI agent you mentioned—that Rutland guy—is looking for you in connection with his investigation of your friend, the cellist."

"I had nothing to do with what happened at the Fourth of July concert. I was just a member of the audience."

"You know that and I know that, but this Rutland is kind of a zealot according to what I hear from my sources. He's trying to get transferred to a better post than Salem, Oregon, and he thinks this bombing is his ticket to stardom. He's casting a wide net, and you may not be able to avoid getting caught in it. You escaped his clutches, and guys like him don't like that."

"I didn't actually 'escape his clutches.' I hadn't been formally questioned, and no one told me I was going to be. This book tour was already scheduled. I don't see how . . ."

"Look, Tom, guys like Caleb Rutland don't deal in the niceties of life. He had you in his sights, and you got away. The reasons don't matter. Call your lawyer and fly home as quickly as you can. You don't want to get charged with obstruction of justice."

"OBSTRUCTION OF JUSTICE! That's crazy! What justice have I obstructed?"

"Tom, calm down and listen to me carefully. These are unusual times. Ever since 9/11, a lot of things that are crazy and unfair and unreasonable have happened to innocent people. We haven't time for me to give you examples. Just get the hell out of New York. I'll keep working on this and try to figure out what Rutland knows. I'll also try to find out more about this guy Andy Hood. Given the people he hangs around with, I doubt that's his real name."

"No kidding," I said.

"I don't get why the guy in the park was looking for you."

I couldn't answer that one.

"Don't tell me—let me guess," he said. "You went looking for Hood in the New York area."

Bickford knew me too well.

"Queens," I said.

"Why doesn't that surprise me."

"I had a lead on where he might be from my lawyer's investigator. I went to a Lebanese restaurant, and some men saw me there. I followed them later in a cab to a warehouse in Brooklyn."

Bickford sighed audibly. "Get the hell out of New York, and I'll be in touch."

"I've booked a flight for . . ."

Bickford hung up before I could finish. I quickly punched in another number.

"Lorenzo. It's Tom. I wasn't sure you'd still be at the office."

"God, Tom. I'm glad you called. I was about to try to contact you. Let me call you right back. Are you where you said you'd be?"

Before I left Oregon, Lorenzo and I had agreed not to reveal where I was staying in case the FBI had put a tap on either of our phones. He had the number of the Hotel Edison so he could reach me using his cell phone without any prying ears listening in.

"Yeah, I am. I'll wait for you to call back."

He did so in two minutes.

"How are you doing, my friend?"

"Okay. Just had my book signing tonight. I'm a bit bummed out because my old girlfriend was there."

"With someone else, I take it?" asked Lorenzo.

"Yeah, someone we both know, but I won't use any names."

"Sorry, pal. I know what you're going through, even though the objects of my affection always wore trousers and had to shave every day."

We both laughed.

"I haven't found out much about the Lebanese connection," I said. "I did see the guy in question briefly. In fact, some guys might be after me because I went to Queens to follow that lead. One tried to stab me."

"STAB YOU?" shouted Lorenzo. "*Dios mio!* Are you okay?"

"Yeah. Fine. My army friend Paul Bickford shot him on the spot."

"Well, great. Just another run-of-the-mill day for your average college professor."

"By this time, I am numb to all this stuff."

"I don't mean to be callous about your narrow escape, but you've got more trouble than having some swarthy guys in oversized suits after you," he said. "Caleb Rutland from the FBI is on your trail. He says you fled the state to avoid being hauled into his investigation."

"Bickford already warned me. Rutland hasn't contacted me that I know of, and I already had this book tour set up," I said. "You told me to disappear for a while."

"You know it and I know it, but he's with the FBI. He's got the badge and the might of the federal government on his side. If you return here by morning, I can argue all that with him. Can you do that?"

"I've already canceled the rest of my book tour. I'm taking the 'red eye' flight out of here tonight. I'll be there."

"Good. I'll check the time and be there to meet you."

* * * * *

At ten that night, I was sitting at a gate in Newark International Airport waiting to board the flight to Portland. I had feigned illness with my agent, and she had agreed to call the four other bookstores on my tour and cancel. I promised to sign copies for them as soon as I could—a popular enticement in bookselling even when the author was not there—and rebook the appearances as soon as I "recovered."

As I was trying to concentrate on that day's issue of *The New York Times,* I noticed two dark-skinned men walk into the waiting room, glance at me, and then pretend they had not done so. My heart began to race, and a few drops of sweat ran down my spine. I read and reread the front page of the paper as I tried to figure out what to do.

The men sat down, and one of them began to talk on a cell phone. I felt somewhat safe because of all the people around me. I did not think they would try anything here. But what about on the plane, especially after the lights went out during the flight? Would my throat be slit while I tried to read?

"Flight 102 for Portland is ready to begin the boarding process at Gate 15A. We will be boarding passengers with small children first, as well as those of you who need a little more time to walk down the passageway to the aircraft. Also, our Diamond Deluxe passengers may board at this time."

A few people in all of those categories got up and formed a line leading to the agent who was checking boarding passes at the gate. I joined them, acquiring a slight limp as I did so. The two men sat motionless as I passed them. My limp got worse as I reached the agent.

"Thank you for letting me board early," I said, with a sad look on my face. "Old war injury." I nodded in the direction of my left knee.

"Oh, you bet," said the perky airline gate attendant. "Thank you for your service." She scanned my boarding pass and tore off the smaller end listing my seat assignment.

I hobbled down the gangway after a woman pushing one of those new giant strollers that needed an instruction manual to operate. Two little toddlers sat quietly in their seats. When we got to the door of the plane, she paused to disassemble this formidable contraption. I ducked around her as both babies started crying loudly.

I nodded at the flight attendant standing by the door and stopped.

"Any chance I could be by an emergency exit? It would give me room for my bum leg. I don't mind assisting in an emergency."

"Funny you should ask. I just told that lady there that she would have to switch. You can take her seat, and she can sit on the aisle."

The flight attendant stepped around a few passengers and spoke to the lady, a pleasant-looking woman who was very overweight. Better to block me from the bad guys. The attendant motioned forward. I hobbled toward the two of them.

"This nice gentleman has agreed to sit by the emergency exit, and you can sit here on the aisle. That seat was not occupied."

"Oh, dearie, that is a fine thing, a fine thing. Thank you, Jesus, for makin' that possible. Thank you, Jesus."

I shook her outstretched hand and swung around her into my seat, putting the shoulder bag I use to carry books and other things I might need in flight under the seat in front of me. I winched in pain as I adjusted my leg.

"Oh, dearie. Were you hurt in some kind of battle?"

"I . . ."

"You know, my poor Edgar was wounded in World War II, and he had a bum leg for many years after that. God rest his soul, he lived with that pain every day for the rest of his life. He was a good provider, though, and he always . . ."

"Ma'am . . ." The flight attendant spoke and motioned toward the line of passengers blocked by the lady.

'Oh, dearie. I am sorry. I just get carried away when I start talkin' about my Edgar. You know we had ten children, all by natural birth. Why, I told him that I just loved havin' kids with . . ."

"Ma'am . . ."

She sat down beside me with a thud. She was soon trying to find both ends of her seat belt. Sadly, they were on the seat underneath her ample body.

"Can you just raise yourself a bit so I can pull out the belt?" I asked.

"Oh, dearie. I can sure try."

She leaned forward and did a slight jerk upward. I yanked and managed to pull out the end of the belt nearest me. The other side would be more of a problem. I leaned across her as she tried the same maneuver. I yanked, but the belt would not budge. I made one more frantic pull, and the belt broke free. In the process, however, my face landed right in her ample bosom.

"Well now, dearie. I don't think we know each other that well."

We both laughed as I disentangled myself from the folds of her dress. In doing so, I loosened the large brooch that was pinned dead center, and it slid down between her breasts.

"Oh, my," she said loudly. "That felt very good!"

I felt my face turn red as I leaned back in my seat and fastened my own seat belt. It was going to be a long flight, I thought, but this nice lady would be protecting me, whether she knew it or not.

＊　＊　＊　＊　＊

I dozed off and on during the night, trying desperately to keep the head of my seatmate from lolling over onto my shoulder. I tried to put the thought of the two Middle Eastern men out of my mind. I was sure that my new friend—Cordelia Mayhew—would raise a fuss if they disturbed either of us.

When we landed in Portland just after 3 a.m., I waited for the two men to disembark. They did so in the first wave of passengers getting off and did not look in my direction as they passed.

"Mrs. Mayhew, I . . ."

"Call me Cordy, if I can call you Tom."

"Of course. Thanks, Cordy. I enjoyed your company. I hope your surgery goes well and that you get your flower garden in."

I gathered my bag and stepped over her. This time, I did not lose my balance and fall into her chest. She patted my hand as I started down the aisle.

As I emerged from the gangway, I could see the two Middle Eastern men embracing wives and many children. If they were terrorists, they had brought a cast of hundreds to greet them at the airport.

What was really troubling, however, was a phalanx of grim-faced men standing in the center of the concourse, with Caleb Rutland at the front.

"Thomas Martindale," he said. "I have instructions from a federal judge to escort you to the United States courthouse to answer a few questions before a federal grand jury tomorrow."

Before I could respond, Lorenzo stepped up to Rutland.

"My client is not to be restrained in any way. I have my own order here that allows him to accompany me to a hotel. As an officer of the court, I have sworn to present him to federal court later this morning. He is not to be held in any kind of custody."

Rutland glanced at the paper and considered it for a moment, then at his signal, his men relaxed and moved away from their positions.

"See you later, professor," he said to me with a smirk. "And you too, counselor." He turned and followed his men through a door marked *No Admittance*.

"Boy, Lorenzo, am I glad to see you!"

We embraced, and I held him for a while and patted him on the back, despite the stares of other passengers as they disembarked.

"You are about the only friend I've got. Thanks for being here."

As we walked toward the exit, I heard a familiar voice beside me.

"Oh, dearie, how nice that your son came to meet you," shouted Cordelia Mayhew, as she sailed past us on one of those fast carts the airport uses for people who can't walk very well.

JULY 12, 2007

LORENZO HAD ALREADY CHECKED US INTO adjoining rooms at a hotel in Lake Oswego near Interstate 5.

"I didn't want to stay downtown where we'd be close to the court-house. I doubt Rutland has the resources to plant bugs in hotels, but you never know," he explained, as we headed into town on I-84. "I'll fill you in on where things stand once we get in the room and you have a shower to wake up. We've got a long night ahead to get you ready for the grand jury. You are due there at 11 a.m.—six hours away."

As we sped along the deserted freeway, Lorenzo told me that Rutland had returned my computer to him, and he had sent a tech-nician to my house to set it up. Then he asked me to fill him in on what had happened in New York. I told him about going to the Lebanese restaurant, the guys I followed in the cab, and the attack on Bickford and me in Paley Park.

"All of this has made me so paranoid that I thought two Middle Eastern men at Kennedy Airport were part of Andy Hood's gang."

He laughed. "Listen to you," he said. "You sound like one of those writers for crime magazines."

"I doubt those old pulps even exist any more," I said, shaking my head. "They're probably crime blogs now, written by both cops and criminals."

Lorenzo was quiet for a few miles, and I dozed off.

"Andy Hood," he said, waking me with a start, although I pretended I hadn't been asleep. "Tom, are you awake?"

"Me? Awake? Yeah, of course."

"Hood has got to be an alias."

"Paul Bickford is trying to find out more about him beyond the lead to that building in Queens where I went," I said, rubbing my tired eyes. "That only got me into more trouble."

We lapsed into silence after that, and I dozed off again until we arrived at the hotel.

✳ ✳ ✳ ✳ ✳

Lorenzo was all set up to prepare me for my appearance before the grand jury. The extra bed was covered with boxes of folders. He had placed a white board on the desk, on which he had written a timeline of what had happened at the bridge on the Fourth of July. Because he would not be able to accompany me into the room, he needed to make sure that I answered the questions without hesitation, and that I did not offer more information than was asked for.

"I guess that is the essence of grand jury testimony—or any testimony in any courtroom," he explained, as we sat down together in his room after I had showered and shaved. "Answer the questions truthfully, but don't go beyond that. Lawyers are trained to move in for the kill if you do."

"Right. I get it. No blabbering." I picked out an apple from a bowl on a table and poured a cup of coffee.

"And you'd better quit drinking that stuff or you'll have to pee and you won't be able to," he laughed.

"I've been thinking about those poor people who were in the car that went over the side."

"Yeah, a couple and their two kids," he said.

"Tough. Wrong place, wrong time."

"Exactly, and that is precisely where you find yourself, my good friend. A chain of events put you right at the scene, near a woman who died on stage. And you are what the feds call a 'close associate' of the woman who is considered the ringleader of a terrorist conspiracy."

"That is absolutely nuts," I said. "No way is Michaela a terrorist. You've met her. You've seen that she is too gentle a soul to be involved with terrorists or bomb plots—or murder. I suppose Agent Rutland is trying to pin Sheila Cross's death on her too."

"Not that I know of," he said. "That is being handled by the Sheriff's Office and the Oregon State Police as a separate matter."

"And I haven't been dragged into that?"

"Not so far. They are looking at the former husband and the jealousy angle."

"I met him, and he seemed like a mild-mannered guy who was distraught over the death of his wife," I said. "It's disconcerting how people's lives can be disrupted and turned into a nightmare in an instant."

"Yeah," he said. "Very sad. But you will be worse than sad if you aren't prepared for the grand jury. Let's focus on that now."

"Right, I get it. Focus, focus, focus!"

"Okay, here we go." Lorenzo walked over to the white board and started writing on it with a black dry marker pen.

I. *Michaela Ross as terrorist*
   1. *Mother was Lebanese*
   2. *Middle name is Rashida*
   3. *Studied at American University in Beirut, summer 1980*
   4. *Known to frequent Lebanese restaurants in several cities*
   5. *Fingerprint found on shell casing*

II. *Thomas Martindale as terrorist wannabe*
1.   *Seen frequently with Michaela Ross*
2.   *Seen taking notes during these encounters*
3.   *Present at Fourth of July concert at Coast Guard station*
4.   *Seen pointing at bridge before shelling*
5.   *Leaves town soon after bridge attack*
6.   *Returns reluctantly to Oregon*

"You have got to be kidding me," I said, my voice rising. "This is all totally fabricated."

"Keep it down, Tom," said Lorenzo, lowering his hand to signal quiet. "It's the middle of the night."

"This is all so flimsy and circumstantial. I can't see how it won't be laughed out of court."

"You know that and I know that, but you're forgetting the climate of fear the government has so successfully created and kept alive since 9/11. If anyone opposes their policies, they wave the Patriot Act and everyone falls into line. It's scary, but it happens all the time. And that is how this applies to you. Everything is trumped up except the fingerprint. That is tangible evidence, and that is what may land your friend Michaela in prison for a very long time."

"I keep forgetting about her. How is she? I should have asked before."

"About like you'd expect if you'd been in jail for over a week and not been able to see anyone but yours truly."

"Any chance for bail?"

"Not so far. The U.S. Attorney in Portland is an old buddy of Rutland's, and he has been successful so far in blocking bail while the FBI gathers more evidence."

"God, what a crock!"

"It is that, indeed," he said. "Now, let's focus on what they will ask you, and what you will say."

And we did just that for the next two hours, until I could not think—or see—straight. Lorenzo let me sleep for two hours after that. Then I got up, showered again, and dressed in my best suit— blue pinstriped with a tie to match and a pale blue shirt—which he had brought from my house. We ate breakfast delivered by room service and were ready to go. I noticed that Lorenzo had dressed for success too and was resplendent in a gray, pinstriped suit set off by a white shirt and yellow tie, with matching handkerchief protruding from the jacket pocket. We could well have been a couple of fashion models for a men's magazine. On second thought, maybe only Lorenzo would fit into that category.

✳ ✳ ✳ ✳ ✳

Among the people milling around in the hall outside the grand jury room was Caleb Rutland, who was looking particularly pleased. I suppose he would be testifying after I did. Lorenzo led me to a bench as far away from him as possible, but Rutland walked over to us anyway.

"Professor Martindale, good to see you looking so rested this morning after your long flight last night," he said, offering his hand.

Lorenzo stepped between us before I could reply.

"My client does not need any distractions, Agent Rutland. He needs to focus on his testimony. I'm sure you would not want to impede that in any way, being the valiant upholder of the law that you are."

Rutland got red in the face and stepped as close as he could to Lorenzo without stepping on his highly polished shoes.

"Don't push me too far, counselor. The federal judicial system has ways to deal with attorneys, as well as their guilty-as-hell clients!"

"Funny, Agent Rutland, I thought the grand jury would be determining that this afternoon after hearing from my client. I guess we'd better talk to the U.S. Attorney about calling off the session. They need to know that their work is already done."

"Watch your back, counselor," hissed Rutland in reply. "We know all about you and your perverted sexual activities."

Lorenzo looked startled for a moment, then regained his composure.

"Last time I looked at the Constitution, it didn't say anything about one's sexual orientation having anything to do with rights of citizenship. I have never tried to hide the fact that I am gay and proud of it." He turned his back on Rutland and sat down beside me.

"Just be very careful—both of you," the agent said before walking toward a group of men at the other end of the hall.

"What was *that* all about, Lorenzo?" I asked.

"That was a case of an FBI agent who seems to be going a bit off the rails," he said. "That was intimidation, no question about it."

"Can you do anything about it?"

"I'm not sure I want to just now. But I'll keep it in the drawer for later, if I need it. Of course, the two of us are the only ones who heard what he said, and he will deny it. But, I can still embarrass him and the bureau by bringing it up."

At that moment, the big wooden doors of the jury room opened and a short, dumpy woman emerged.

"Thomas Martindale," she said a bit more loudly than I would have wished, her voice a cross between a town crier and a barker at a sideshow.

Both Lorenzo and I stood up, and he patted me on the back and whispered, "Focus on what they ask and tell the truth, and you will be fine. I'll be waiting for you right here."

I followed the woman into the room and a large, beefy man—presumably a federal marshal with the requisite shaved head—closed the door behind me. The woman pointed to a chair at a table in front of two rows of chairs on a slightly elevated platform. The chairs were occupied by the men and women of the jury. A judge—looking down at the proceedings with a stern expression on his face—sat behind a large bench on a raised platform in the front of the room.

All eyes seemed to be on me as I sat down. I quickly poured water from a pitcher sitting there into a glass and drank a couple swallows. To my right stood a man I would not have picked out of a crowd as a U.S. Attorney. He was in his forties and dressed rather flashily—a plaid suit and lavender striped shirt with a tie that could only be described as "jungle-like" with animals and a lot of foliage. His hair was also a lot longer than what I expected was the norm, so much so that I suspected he had to tie it back when he did anything very strenuous to keep it out of his eyes. I could also imagine that he might add a stud or two to his earlobe in his off-hours.

"Good morning, Mr. Martindale," said the man. "Thank you for coming. My name is Danny Lee Draper, and I am an assistant United States Attorney.

"You're welcome."

A loud screech filled the room.

"Please move the mike away from you and be sure to speak directly into it," Draper instructed me.

"Sorry."

"Please state your name and city of residence and your occupation."

"Thomas Edwin Martindale. I live in Newport, Oregon. I am currently a professional writer and am on leave without pay from Oregon University in Corvallis where I'm a professor of journalism."

"Thank you, Mr. Martindale. Or should I call you professor?"

"Either one is fine."

"We are here to investigate the events that occurred on July 4th of this year in Newport, Oregon," said Draper. "Are you aware of what happened in that city on that day?"

"Yes, sir, I am."

"Please tell the jury your understanding of those occurrences."

I cleared my throat and suddenly needed another sip of water. I took my time to swallow it before beginning.

"On the Fourth of July, I was attending an outdoor concert, which is put on every year by the Oregon Coast Symphony Orchestra to celebrate the holiday. This year, it was held at the United States Coast Guard station in Newport. I attended the concert, as I say, and had a good seat near the front."

"And from the vantage point of that seat, what could you see?"

"I saw the orchestra and the waters of Yaquina Bay and the bridge over that bay . . ."

"That bridge is called what?"

"The Yaquina Bay Bridge. It is one of the iconic bridges along the Oregon coast and has stood there since the 1930s."

"I think we can dispense with the history lesson, professor." Draper had a testy side.

"Sorry. I guess I am always on duty as a teacher."

Several jurors smiled and nodded their heads.

"If we could stay on point, sir, I would appreciate it. We have only so much time here." More of Draper's testiness, which I probably should not arouse. I smiled and nodded.

"What happened next?"

"Near the end of the concert, as the orchestra was finishing the *1812 Overture* by Tchaikovsky, several large guns began to be fired from the park across the bay under the bridge."

"And was this startling and unusual?"

"No, the composer included that element in his original piece. The cannons are part of the concert, almost like musical instruments. You see, the symphony commemorates Napoleon's defeat in his invasion of Russia, so these are meant to signify the guns of battle. Later, there are church bells to signify the victory of the Russians over . . ."

"Thank you, professor, I think we get the drift," Draper said impatiently. "Did the gunfire go well that night?"

"To a point, but then one of the shells appeared to go off course."

"And what happened then? Please tell us."

"It hit the bridge with a loud crash and flashes of explosive. As we watched in horror, a car drove off the bridge and cascaded downward into the water of the bay."

"And then, what did you and others do?"

"We were silent for a few seconds, and then many people screamed and stood up and started running away from the orchestra, I presume to the exits."

"And what did you do, professor?"

"The orchestra kept playing for a few minutes because I guess neither the conductor nor anyone else knew what had happened. Then they stopped. I could see a friend of mine in the orchestra look to her left, and then I heard her scream."

"And that friend would be? . . ."

"Her name is Michaela Ross. She is a cellist in the orchestra."

"For the record, that person is named Michaela RASHIDA Ross, who is a person currently under investigation in this case."

I found it disconcerting that Draper was putting a strong emphasis on Michaela's Arabic-sounding middle name.

"Could you determine why she was screaming?" asked Draper.

"At first, I thought it was because of the explosion and the sight of the car falling off the bridge."

"And that was not the reason?"

"No, she had looked over to the cellist next to her and saw that the woman had slumped in her chair and that blood was oozing down her face."

"And that person was named? . . ."

"Sheila Cross."

"What happened next, professor? Please continue."

"By this time, other people had run up onto the stage and several were trying to help Ms. Cross and Michaela."

"That would be Michaela Rashida Ross, who is under investigation in this case."

"Yes, but she did not have anything . . ."

"I am asking the questions here, Professor Martindale," said Draper impatiently. "Please refrain from adding your observations or anything I do not ask you about."

"I just thought . . ."

"Your task here is not to think about anything except what I asked you," he said heatedly. "Is that clear?"

I wished that Lorenzo was beside me to object, but he was not. It felt like Draper was badgering me to hide things I knew to be true.

"Yes, it is." I bit my lip to keep from apologizing. I did not want to appear even more submissive to these jurors than I probably already did.

"You were talking about the scene on the stage immediately after the artillery shell hit the bridge."

"As I was saying, others came to the stage to render assistance to the injured."

"And who were these individuals?"

"One was Sheila Cross's former husband, Ted May. He ran over to her and held her head in his hands, sobbing and moaning. The other man was a tall bass player—I think his name is Matt—who looked after Michaela."

"You do not have a last name for him?"

"No, I only heard his first name. You should be able to get . . ."

"Thank you, professor. I am sure we already have it in our files."

Then why did you ask me if you already knew, I thought to myself. I nodded at Draper.

"What were you doing at this time?"

"I was talking to Monk Beasley, the commander of the U.S.

Coast Guard station in Newport. He was the host for the concert and, because of its location on federal property, he was in charge of making sure that the property was secure, that everyone was safe, and, I suppose, that nothing else there posed any danger to his troops and to the civilians who were still in the area."

"What did he tell you?"

"That the shell had come from one of the guns on the other side, fired as planned during the concert. That the person who fired the cannon was not known at that time. Things like that."

"Did he advise you to do anything yourself?"

I did not like where this was going, for Monk's sake.

"I don't follow."

"Did he alert you about your own status?"

"Not that I recall."

Draper smiled and picked up what looked like a transcript from the table next to the podium where he had been standing.

"Did he not say, 'This place is going to be crawling with *federales,* and you'd better get out of here and take your friend with you'—or words to that effect?"

"Oh, yeah, I guess he did say something like that," I said rather sheepishly. "It was pretty confusing at that point. I am a bit hazy on everything that happened in those few minutes."

Draper smiled again and put the transcript down. He and his investigators had done their work well. I was surprised that anyone had heard my brief conversation with Monk that night.

"I hope we won't find other instances where your memory has failed you," he said.

It did not take a law degree to figure out that Draper was pulling me into a trap so that anything I said would be tainted in the eyes of these jurors.

"I am a truthful person, Mr. Draper. I think memory is a transitory thing. I'll bet you yourself forget things at . . ."

"But we aren't here to delve into my powers of memory are we, professor?"

"No, I guess we aren't."

"Tell us what happened next."

"I made sure that Michaela Ross was being taken care of by the paramedics who arrived, and then I went home."

"You did not actually take her home?"

"No, I did not. I presume—but do not know for sure—that her friend Matt, the bass player, did so."

"And when did you see her next?"

"I have not seen or talked with her since that night, I guess maybe two weeks ago."

Draper looked surprised. For once, he did not have any notes to contradict what I was saying.

"I tried to call her several times the next day but only got her answering machine. Later, I found out from Commander Beasley that she had been arrested . . ."

"No arrest warrant has been issued for her," said Draper in the tone of a schoolmaster correcting a clueless student.

"Well, then, I guess held for questioning."

"Yes, that is correct. She is being held as a material witness in the incident at the Yaquina Bay Bridge."

He leafed through his notes before looking at me again.

"Did there come a time a few days later when you left Newport?"

"Yes, I did leave town."

"And where did you go?"

Again, Draper was trying to make me look suspicious. How to avoid his traps? I recalled that Lorenzo had told me to keep my answers short and to stick to the questions, never going beyond them. Like many people, I always have had the tendency to fill any void in conversation with my own prattle. This time, I needed to be terse.

"I drove to Salem."

"And why did you go to Salem?"

"To visit a friend."

"And that friend would be? . . ."

"Lorenzo Madrid."

"And is he more than a friend?"

"I am not sure what you mean by the question, Mr. Draper."

"Isn't Mr. Madrid your attorney?"

Would Draper bring out details of my arrest for murder a few years ago—an arrest that was trumped up? Thanks to Lorenzo, I had been freed the next morning. Even a hint of that incident would taint me in the eyes of the jury even more. I seemed to recall that prior acts like that would not be admissible in a trial. Did that same rule apply in a grand jury proceeding?

"Yes, he is my attorney, but he is also a friend."

"And why did you feel the need to see him at this time?"

I felt confident in shading the truth a bit here. Draper could not compel Lorenzo to say anything he did not want to say about me. As my attorney, Lorenzo was bound by the attorney-client relationship.

"I was going out of town, and he offered to let me stay with him on my way to the airport in Portland."

"So, you were leaving town in a hurry for parts unknown." Draper was smirking.

"Not 'parts unknown.' I knew where I was going."

Several jurors smiled at my slight interjection of humor. For his part, however, Draper was not amused.

"Save the jokes for the classroom, professor. Where were you going so hastily?"

"I was on my way to New York to begin a book tour to publicize my new book."

"Was that tour put together at the last minute?"

"You mean so I would have an excuse to leave town?" Might

as well move things along to let the jurors know that I knew what Draper was getting at.

"Yes, I guess I do mean that."

"The tour had been scheduled a week before the Fourth of July concert. I was to go to New York, Chicago, Denver, and Los Angeles, in that order. All on the up and up. You can check with my agent, who set it up, and my publisher, Flatiron Press in New York. I can give you names and contact information if you wish."

Draper looked a bit dismayed that he had not been able to impeach my credibility.

"I don't think that will be necessary. We can move on to another line of inquiry. Is it not true that you cut this tour short and returned to Oregon?"

"Yes, that's right, I did. I arrived back in Portland early this morning."

"I am surprised that you would halt this tour that had been so carefully planned by your agent and publisher."

"I think you know, Mr. Draper, that I was advised by my attorney, Mr. Madrid, to return because of my appearance here this morning." I smiled at the jurors to assuage any impression that I resented having to come here. Several of them smiled and nodded at me, gestures Draper noticed.

"Do you consider yourself a loyal American?"

What kind of a question was that? Was Draper now going to go for a terrorist link? If all else fails, play the disloyalty card.

"Yes, Mr. Draper, I do. I love this country, and I would never do anything to dishonor it or harm it. I must say I resent what you are..."

"Just thought I would ask, in view of your friendship with Michaela Rashida Ross."

Finally, we were getting to the crux of all this palaver. Like academics, lawyers are good at dancing around what they really want to know.

"I am not sure what you want to know."

"You have been friends with her for some time?"

"No, only a few months."

"And how did you come to know her?"

"I met her because I wanted to find out about an opening on the board of the Oregon Coast Symphony Orchestra."

"And did you eventually join that board?"

"No, I did not. I decided I needed the time to work on several book projects."

"But you still saw Michaela Rashida Ross frequently. Were you romantically involved with her?"

"No, nothing like that. Ms. Ross and I are just good friends."

"So, why did you see her again?"

"Look, counselor, I'm not sure where you are going with this, but I fail to see how my friendship with Michaela Ross or anyone else has any bearing on what we are discussing here this morning."

Draper held up his hand to cut me off.

"I remind you that you are under oath and testifying before a federal grand jury," he said heatedly. "You cannot take these meandering sojourns that avoid my questions."

"Sorry, Mr. Draper. I saw Ms. Ross several more times because I was interviewing her for a profile I plan to write and include in a collection of my journalistic pieces scheduled to come out next year. I am updating some old articles I wrote early in my career as a journalist and then adding a few new ones. One of them will be about Ms. Ross."

"And why pick her? Was it her Middle Eastern background?"

There it was: the essence of Draper's attempt to taint the jurors and plant the seed that Michaela Ross was an Islamic terrorist.

"I was not aware of Ms. Ross's ethnic background," I said. "I was interested in her as a concert cellist. She talked to me about her background and how a musician of her ability performs as part of a world-class symphony orchestra."

"I am no music expert, but I doubt that the Oregon Coast Symphony Orchestra would be called 'world class'," said Draper with one of his characteristic smirks.

"I was referring to the Oregon Symphony Orchestra, in which Ms. Ross performed for thirty-five years before her retirement."

Draper looked flustered and thumbed through his notes. "I guess I missed that bit of information," he said. "So, you met only to interview her. How many times did these meetings take place?"

Draper made our casual interviews sound like the gathering of a bunch of subversives.

"We had two INTERVIEWS over several weeks," I replied, raising my voice to emphasize the one word. "Then I attended the Fourth of July concert, mostly to see her perform, but also to learn how the orchestra went about playing complicated pieces of music. It is not as easy as it looks."

"Save your editorial comments for your article, Professor Martindale."

Draper's increasingly snotty tone was not lost on several of the jurors. One woman in the front row seemed to resent the attorney and glared at him several times when he seemed to be picking on me. Once, I thought I saw her shake her head ever so slightly at his outrageousness.

"I don't think I have any more questions for you, professor." He turned to the jurors. "Does anyone on the panel have anything to ask the good professor?"

"So, you did not know she was from the Middle East before you interviewed her?" asked a short, older man sitting in the second row.

"No, sir, I did not," I said. "But I was not talking to her about her family background. I was talking to her about music and her playing the cello."

Thinking back, I guess Michaela had mentioned that her

mother was Lebanese, but it was no more pertinent than if she had said that her mother came from Nebraska.

"And you did not leave the state to get away from anyone investigating the bridge bombing?" asked a young woman with blond hair sitting at the end of the first row. She was dressed as a Dolly Parton wannabe wearing a tight skirt and a sequined top that put her breasts on prominent display. The older man who had asked the first question could not keep his eyes from peeking at her from his vantage point in the row behind her.

"No, ma'am, I did not. As I said, my book tour was arranged long before the bridge bombing, and I was just following already made plans. When these things are set up, I feel duty bound not to let people down who are expecting me to appear. I mean, publicity is put out, bookstores order books, and . . ."

"Thank you, Mr. Martindale," said Draper. "We don't need a primer on how authors conduct their book tours."

"I, for one, am interested in such details."

All eyes turned to the lady who had seemed so peeved at Draper earlier. I knew I had her vote, if no one else's.

"In fact, people have always told me that I should tell my story. I would hope that Mr. Martindale would help me find a publisher. It begins when my great-grandparents traveled to Oregon in a covered wagon from . . ."

Draper rushed over and stood in front of her.

"THAT IS NOT WHY WE ARE HERE, MADAME!" He was shouting and getting red in the face. I sat back and smiled to myself. His outburst probably made a few more jurors sympathetic to me. The woman glared but said nothing more.

"If there are no further questions, I am ready to dismiss this witness," said Draper. "You will be notified in due course if we have any desire to talk to you further, Mr. Martindale. You may go, but be sure your attorney's phone number is on file with the court clerk."

I nodded to Draper and to the woman who was my supporter before turning around and walking out of the room. Lorenzo was waiting for me outside.

"How did it go, Tom?"

"I don't know much about sports lingo, but I would say that it was a slam dunk."

JULY 13, 2007

EVEN THOUGH LORENZO HAD TOLD ME TO GO HOME and get on with my life, I found it hard to get back to my writing routine the next morning. For one thing, I was worried about whether the Middle Eastern men who had been after me in New York would turn up here, as unlikely as that seemed. After all, the so-called "Andy Hood" had been here and, no doubt, carried out the attack on the bridge. For another, I was concerned that my testimony had somehow hurt Michaela. There were just too many loose ends.

I took the cell phone Lorenzo had given me for the trip and stepped outside. I walked along the bluff, sniffing the sea air. It was a glorious morning without the typical summer fog that the heat in the valley often pulls in. For me, the ocean was kind of a "near and yet so far" kind of thing. I loved living next to it, but too often I convinced myself that I did not have time to meander along the beach, even though I always felt better when I did.

I reached the top of a cove that had been the location of a particularly bad incident several years ago. A beached whale had been the focal point for a gruesome murder, and I had been involved in discovering the killer. This morning, however, the cove was empty and spectacular, as waves from the sea crashed through an opening in the rocks. No one dared to venture here except at low tide lest they be crushed against the rocks and carried out to sea. In fact, that is exactly what had happened before.

I punched in a now familiar number, less apprehensive than I had been before.

"Menzies and March Photo Agency."

I paused to make sure my voice did not sound nervous.

"Hello? . . ."

"Hello, Maxine. It's Tom."

"Yes, Tom. How can I help you?" Civilized and correct, but nothing warm in her tone. What did I expect? I answered the same way—or tried to.

"I was trying to reach Paul. He was looking into some stuff for me, and I wondered what he had found out."

"He isn't here, Tom. You know he doesn't live here, and you know how secretive he is. He does what he does and only drops by here when he is in New York. I will tell him you called if and when I hear from him. That's all I can promise." Her voice was getting more correct and colder by the minute.

"Thanks, Maxine. I appreciate it."

"If there's nothing else, I've got to . . ."

"No, that's what I wanted. I'll try to figure out another way to reach him in the future."

"Good idea. Goodbye, Tom."

"Before you hang up, I wanted to say that I appreciated you coming to my book signing. It was good to see you again."

There was silence on the line for several seconds. I hoped she was about to say something nice.

"Good luck with your book, Tom. I know how hard you work. Goodbye."

She disconnected so fast that I was left still holding the cell phone to my ear. I said goodbye in return even though I knew I was speaking into dead air. I walked back to my house with the knowledge that Maxine March would never be a part of my life again.

* * * * *

I spent the rest of the morning doing laundry and cleaning my house, which I had badly neglected because of my trip and the chaotic events before I left. I had finished lunch when my cell phone buzzed.

"Hello."

"Turn off your phone and go outside to the bluff and start walking south."

I obeyed the familiar voice. When I reached the area above the cove, the phone buzzed again.

"Yes, Paul."

"Now I want you to drive to the Yaquina Bay Bridge and meet me in the parking lot of the park next to it. Know where that is?"

"I'll be there in ten minutes."

* * * * *

I had not been in Newport for over a week, and I wondered how the disruption of traffic on Highway 101—the only way to drive north and south along the Oregon coast—was affecting the town. From what I could see this morning, things seemed to be back to normal. The summer deluge of motor homes and pickups pulling boats seemed normal. Those of us who live here know the vital role that visitors play in the local economy, yet we hate the delays caused by their presence on the highway.

I took a shortcut along the water that took me by Agate Beach and through the old section of town called Nye Beach. I followed the road around the Performing Arts Center and then drove past the big hotels. I turned into the grounds of the Yaquina Bay State Park and drove to the parking lot below the lighthouse. Police tape blocked further passage along the normal route under the bridge.

The tourists were once again being allowed to get out of their cars and walk up the hill to the lighthouse or look out onto where the jetty marked the entrance to the bay. The waters of the bay and the ocean beyond were choppy this afternoon.

This had long been one of the most treacherous sections of the coast. Many ships had gone aground and their crews killed this close to shore in the cauldron that was created when fresh water and seawater come together.

I parked my car and walked up to a sheriff's deputy who was standing next to the cordon.

"I'm supposed to meet a federal officer here."

"Your name, sir?"

"Tom Martindale," I said, as I pulled out my driver's license and handed it to him.

"Hmmm. Name sounds familiar." He thought for a moment, then handed my license back to me.

"I'm a writer. Maybe you've seen my name in the paper."

No need to bring up the real reason for his hazy recollection. I am sure my name had been bandied about among the former sheriff's troopers. His death a year ago had revealed his acceptance of bribes from a Mexican drug dealer. The whole force must have felt disgraced. And I had brought it all out into the open.

The deputy spoke into the microphone attached to a strap on his shoulder.

"There's a man here looking for that federal guy I let in about an hour ago." He listened and smiled at me. "The guy you want is over there." He pointed toward a group of men walking up the hill from under the bridge.

"Funny," said the deputy, "I don't even know his name."

Why wasn't I surprised that the super-cautious Paul Bickford would remain anonymous?

"Thanks for your help."

I ducked under the tape and walked toward the men. Bickford broke away from them when he saw me, as did Monk Beasley.

"God help us all if you two are putting your heads together," I laughed.

"How've you been?" said Monk, hugging me and patting me on the back. "I hear you've been away."

Bickford was decidedly less congenial. "Tom." We shook hands only briefly.

The two of them glanced at each other, then Bickford led me toward a bridge piling.

"I've got a lot to do this morning," said Beasley, over his shoulder, as he walked away, "but we're long overdue for lunch. Call me when you have time. Linda sends her love and so does Jessie." Both his wife, Linda, and their Labrador retriever had been special to me for a long time.

"I promise," I replied.

Bickford and I stopped walking when we were safely out of earshot of everyone else in the area. The other men had gone to their cars and were departing anyway.

"So, what's happening here?" I said, looking up at the top of the bridge. You could see where the hole in the side rail had been, but it was patched with steel mesh and plywood.

"I'm told that the roadway was not hit by the shell, thank God," he said, "only the railing. Of course, that left an opening large enough for the one car to fall through. The highway department is letting traffic through one lane at a time. It would be best to keep it closed until major repairs are finished, but that isn't possible with Highway 101. It just disrupts everything too badly."

"Don't I know it," I said, shaking my head. "I've lived through many closures over the years, and it causes real hassles for everyone. I'm surprised to see you here. Why'd they send you out?"

"Nice to see you too, Tom."

Bickford's testiness was unexpected. Maybe he was feeling uncomfortable about his involvement with Maxine and how I felt about it. I was not going to go anywhere near that subject, of course.

"I didn't mean I'm not glad you're here, I just figured you'd be someplace more exotic than Newport, Oregon."

Bickford smiled at that remark.

"Yeah, I see your point," he said. "I was sent because the artillery shell came from an army cannon. We need to know that the shooter was acting alone and not part of a larger conspiracy. Since I had worked out here before at various times, my bosses thought I'd meet less resistance from locals than your average investigator from D.C."

"How's the FBI going to react to you nosing around? Have you met Caleb Rutland? He's a real shithead."

"Not yet," said Bickford. "I guess he was busy detaining you in Portland when I arrived. I'll need to pay him a courtesy call and tell him about my mission. I need to make sure he doesn't feel threatened. I am not about to step on his toes. For one thing, I don't have the manpower to do very much. I plan to just ask questions and see what I can find out, mostly about the shooter."

"Andy Hood."

Bickford nodded his head. "I put some feelers out on him. What do you know about him? You mentioned looking for him in Queens when we met in New York. Of course, the guy we encountered in the park . . ."

"The one you shot."

"Yeah, him. He was Middle Eastern, I presume Lebanese. I didn't kill him, you know. What I shot him with was not a bullet but a tranquilizer dart. He woke up after twenty minutes or so with a bad headache but nothing else."

"That is a relief," I said. "Even though he tried to stab me, I thought shooting him in cold blood in a public place was a bit extreme, even for you." I kept my face serious before breaking into a big smile. So did Bickford.

"That shows that someone did not like you nosing around in Queens," he said.

"No kidding. I didn't tell you everything that happened that day."

"Why doesn't that surprise me," he said.

"We did have a pretty rude interruption, Paul. Then I left town."

"Yeah, yeah, whatever. It'll do me no good to tell you to keep your nose out of things like this. Someday you'll get your ass in such a tight sling that even I won't be able to get you out of it."

I told Bickford about following the men from the restaurant to the warehouse and how they were not very happy to see me. I also mentioned my worry about the two men who boarded the plane in New York.

"I made friends with a talkative and rather heavyset lady who sat on the aisle and would have protected me if they tried to get to me during the flight," I continued. "But they were harmless. They left the airport with their wives and children."

"Maybe they were family members or maybe they wanted you to think they were family members," he said. "At least they didn't try anything at the airport."

"They wouldn't have stood a chance with Agent Rutland and some of his men waiting for me at the gate," I said.

"So that restaurant is a meeting place of some sort for Middle Eastern men who had some involvement in this bridge incident here. Maybe it's a sleeper cell of some kind."

"With Andy Hood as the ring leader."

"His name is not 'Andy Hood,' Tom."

"I thought you hadn't found out anything about him," I said.

"He is really Abdul Hakim," he said, ignoring me. "He is a native of Syria who grew up in Lebanon the son of a wealthy businessman. He went to school in the United States and kept his nose clean, for the most part. Two years ago, however, he quit college here and transferred to a university in Damascus. We lost track of him after that."

"How did he wind up here of all places and in the Oregon National Guard?"

"That, my friend, is the main reason I am here. At this point, I have no idea. Presumably, he returned on a student visa and got lost in the boondocks of your fine state. It's not hard to do that, you know. This is a big country, and it's fairly easy to move around under the radar. I guess he forged papers to get into the Guard and was good at firing cannons from where we are standing."

"It gives me kind of an eerie feeling," I said, looking up at the bridge. "What he did was bad, but it could have been worse."

"Much worse, no question about it."

"So, what's next?" I asked.

"I need to try to figure out how our friend Mr. Hakim got into the unit and got assigned to fire that cannon."

"Why isn't the FBI looking into that part of the story? They've got the people to do that."

"Knowing what I know about the bureau from many years of working with its people and observing their approach from the outside, my guess is that your friend . . ."

"Michaela Ross."

"Yes, Ms. Ross. She was an easy target once they found her fingerprint—I think someone told me on a shell casing? With the focus on using the Patriot Act to stop terrorism, the bureau saw a chance to score points with their bosses by using provisions of that law. You have no idea how much pressure there's been over the past few years to arrest people and indict them, just to show that the government is doing something."

"Never mind if innocent people are accused unjustly and their lives are ruined," I said.

"You said it, Tom. I didn't," he said. But I wouldn't disagree. I've spent my entire adult life in the service of this country, and I'm ashamed of the things we're doing under the guise of fighting terrorism and terrorists. I am really ashamed."

I glanced around and lowering my voice said, "Should you be saying these things in public, Paul? Your career could be over if anyone heard you and reported it." It felt odd to find myself cautioning Bickford. In the time I had known him, he was always the one trying to get me to keep things to myself.

"Yeah, yeah. Whatever. It just makes me crazy."

"Bush won't be president forever," I said. "Things are bound to get better once someone else is in charge. In the meantime, you need to focus on doing your job and keep your opinions to yourself."

"Yeah, don't I know it. I'd never say any of this to anyone but a close friend like you."

I was both surprised and touched by what Bickford said. He had never been so candid or as personal before.

"It goes without saying, but I'll say it anyway: your secret is safe with me. I would never betray our friendship or reveal what we say to each other."

"I know, I know," he said. "Thanks. In this case, you need to save me from myself."

"If you find anything to implicate Hakim or Hood or whatever his name is, that'll help my friend get off the hook. Keep me posted."

"So, you're still going to stay involved with her and her case," he asked, "even though it's brought you nothing but grief?"

"You know me, Paul. I can't let things drop. Besides, I'm working on a story about Michaela, and this'll be a part of it. I need to follow this through to an outcome."

Bickford didn't say anything for a few minutes.

"I probably shouldn't tell you this because of your feelings about Maxine, but I will anyway. She has said more than once that she will never forget how much you helped her get through all that business with her former husband. She says you saved her life."

I was grateful for this revelation. I had figured that Maxine hated me. Period.

"Paul, you're the one who saved her life—I mean, rescued her with those troops from that sanitarium in the mountains and got her into the Witness Protection Program and set her up with that photographer, Constantine Menzies. You saved her life and then gave her a new one."

"Yeah, that's true, but I'm just telling you how she looks at it."

"Well, it's nice to hear."

I had no intention of using this tiny bit of praise from Maxine to mend our relationship. I didn't have the stomach to go for that.

"Okay. So we will keep each other informed. You asked me earlier about my helping Michaela. I got Lorenzo to be her attorney, and I want to help get her released from confinement. She has a hearing in a few days, and I'm going to do more research for him while he gets ready to go to court for her."

"You conducting research in a nice, safe library somewhere," he laughed. "That's what I like to hear. No skulking around and putting yourself in danger. That's my department."

"You have my solemn word on that, Paul."

He began laughing, and his laughter continued as I walked away and got into my car.

WHEN I GOT HOME I HAD A BRIEF E-MAIL MESSAGE from
Lorenzo. Given our worry that the FBI had bugged my phone, we
decided to communicate by e-mail, hoping that that means of communication was not compromised too. Any phone calls would be
over new cell phones from locations outside my house and his office.

> *Going to Portland today to see our friend. Trying to set her next
> hearing. I really need that material on fingerprints. Adios, amigo.*

Before I left for New York, I had gathered a lot of material—
from both an attorney friend in Newport and the law archives that
Lorenzo had access to—about fingerprints and their use and abuse
in court over the years. I checked the Internet as well, keeping in
mind that it does contain a great deal of inaccurate information.

With a cup of coffee beside me, I started to compile the background material I hoped would help Lorenzo clear Michaela of
all suspicion.

> *A fingerprint is an impression normally made by ink or con-
> taminants transferred from the peaks of friction skin ridges to a
> relatively smooth surface, such as a fingerprint card. These ridges*

*are sometimes known as "dermal ridges" or "dermal papillae."
The term "fingerprint" normally refers to impressions transferred from the pad on the last joint of fingers and thumbs, though
fingerprint cards also typically record portions of the lower joint
area of the fingers (which are also used to effect identifications). .
. . Friction skin ridges on humans are commonly believed to provide traction for grasping objects. In the more than one hundred
years that fingerprints have been examined and compared, no
two areas of friction skin on any two fingers or palms (including
between identical twins) have been found to have the same friction ridge characteristics.*

That last fact was no surprise to me or anyone else who has
spent years watching movies and cop shows on TV. It made solving
crimes relatively easy: get someone's fingerprint on a weapon or at
the scene of a crime, and his or her guilt is established and convic-
tion a certainty.

That was true until 2004, when a Portland attorney was arrested
by the FBI for his suspected involvement in the bombing of four
commuter trains in Madrid. One hundred ninety-one people died
in the attack and over two thousand others were injured. A federal
judge signed the arrest order based on an affidavit by an FBI agent—
supported by an agency fingerprint examiner—which identified
more than fifteen points of identification of the attorney's prints
on file with the U.S. Army and the FBI. The examiner also claimed
to have found what he called a "photographic image" of a print
recovered from a plastic bag containing several detonators found
in a van near the point where three of the trains departed from the
station. The report said that the experts were "100 percent" positive
that they were right in their conclusion.

The problem was that the attorney was nowhere near Madrid
on the date of the bombing. And he could prove it. The FBI agents
ignored his protestations of innocence as they put him in jail and

searched his office and home. He was released nineteen days later after the Spanish National Police linked two prints on the bag to an Algerian man with a police record and a Spanish residency permit. It later turned out that the agency had told the FBI that the prints were probably not the attorney's and that they had no record that he had even been in the country.

In his lawsuit, the Portland attorney said that the FBI continued to investigate him, even after the Spanish police eliminated him as a suspect. He also noted that even though he ranked four on a list of twenty suspects whose prints might have matched those on the plastic bag, he was singled out, in part at least, because of the fact that he is a practicing Muslim and "this knowledge influenced their examination of . . . [his] . . . fingerprints." Agents began to follow him, his wife, and their three children from their home to his law office, the children's school, and their place of worship. The agents also performed repeated so-called "sneak and peek" searches of their home "so incompetently that the FBI left traces of their searches behind, causing the . . . family to be frightened and to believe that they had been burglarized." The agents also placed wiretaps on telephones in the attorney's home and office.

Two years later, the attorney settled his lawsuit against the United States government for $2 million. He also got an apology from the government for the suffering caused by its investigation of him. The agent in charge of the Portland office said he and his agents had followed the Patriot Act in its investigation of him. They had handled the case correctly, he told reporters, although they had used incorrect fingerprint information. "We built this great investigation, but . . . [it was] . . . one built on sand."

In accepting the settlement, the attorney won the right to move forward on his lawsuit to prove that the Patriot Act is unconstitutional. In that lawsuit, the attorney challenges the Patriot Act amendments to the Federal Intelligence Surveillance Act that allow federal agents to circumvent Fourth Amendment probable cause requirements when investigating persons suspected of crimes. It is still making its way through the federal court system.

I paused to consult an almanac as to what the Fourth Amendment actually says. The Fourth Amendment to the U.S. Constitution established the right "of the people to be secure in their persons, houses, papers, and effects, against unreasonable searches and seizures." This can only be done if probable cause is proven and the place to be searched and person or things to be seized is described.

My coffee had long since gotten cold and stale. I got up to stretch my legs and make another pot. While it was brewing, I walked outside to look at the ocean and its waves crashing against the rocks below my house. I drew in a long breath of the wonderful air and my head felt clearer.

Like the Portland attorney who had brought the lawsuit, Michaela had been detained on what seemed to me to be the flimsiest of evidence. As in the other case, her fingerprint had been found on an incriminating object; however, this time the print was not on a plastic bag containing detonators but on a casing from a shell that had been fired at the bridge. And this time, the terrorist attack had not taken place in a faraway European country but in Oregon.

Lorenzo had yet to see the documentation to back up the charges against Michaela, but it seemed, on the surface at least, to be as speculative as in the other case. Lorenzo and I believed in Michaela's innocence. It was up to me to dig up the facts that he could use in court to prove it.

I decided that I would start my search with the only person who had seen the man who called himself "Andy Hood"—the woman at the only car rental agency in the area.

* * * * *

The few times I had rented a car while living on the Oregon coast, I had used Sea Breeze Car Rental on Highway 101. And each time I had dealt with the woman who ran the place, Agnes Montgomery. Agnes was unforgettable with her big hair and blue eyelids and large, chunky jewelry, most of it custom made and expensive. I guess you'd call her look "retro." Regardless of labels, she was one of the nicest people working for a business in Lincoln City.

She looked up from a pile of paperwork on her desk and smiled. "I should know you, but I can't place the name," she said.

"No reason for you to remember," I answered. "I haven't been in for a while. Tom Martindale."

She walked up to the counter and accepted my outstretched hand.

"What do you need today? I've got a nice Chevy Malibu ready to roll out there."

"I don't need a car today. Just a little information. Have you got a minute?"

"Sure, Tom. Why don't you pull up that chair and join me at the desk."

"I think we have a mutual friend," I said.

"And that would be?" said Agnes, suspiciously. She'd probably heard that line many times before.

"Ray Pearl."

Her face softened. "We were an item once." End of subject.

If she remembered telling Pearl earlier about the Middle Eastern man who had rented a car, she had decided not to mention it.

I walked around the counter and sat down, as Agnes poured us both a cup of coffee.

"Okay, shoot. I'm ready for anything you want to ask."

"A few weeks ago, maybe a day or two before the Fourth of July holiday, a man came in and rented a car. He might have used the name of Andy Hood. Would you have a record of that transaction?"

Agnes narrowed her eyes and quit smiling. "Does this have

anything to do with the bombing of the Yaquina Bay Bridge?"

I nodded.

"The FBI told me not to discuss that with anyone. Why do you want to know? You an undercover cop or something?"

Even though I had vowed not to tell anyone but Lorenzo what I was doing, I decided I needed to confide in Agnes, at least enough to get her to tell me what she knew.

"No, nothing like that. Actually, I'm a writer, and I was in the audience at the Coast Guard station listening to the orchestra when the artillery shell hit the bridge."

Agnes seemed to relax a bit, her eyes less suspicious.

"A friend was playing in the orchestra, and she's been arrested because the cops think she had something to do with the bombing. I'm trying to clear her name. It's all unofficial, but I'm doing my best. I wanted to ask you about this Hood guy. But if you feel that you can't answer my questions, I will understand."

In my career as a reporter, this approach usually worked—playing on sympathy, relying on the fact that people usually like me and don't feel threatened by me. Being blunt and demanding is not my style.

"Oh, your poor friend. She must be terrified. I know that little FBI agent scared me to death." She fished in her desk and pulled out a business card. "Caleb Rutland," she said, squinting at the card. "He was like a Nazi. I didn't like him at all."

"Yeah, I've met him. Kind of a nasty guy. If you don't mind my asking, what did he want to know?"

She hesitated, probably recalling the admonition he undoubtedly gave her not to talk about any of this with anyone.

"I need to tell you, Agnes, that anything you tell me is between us. I am after information only. I won't use your name. You have my word on that."

I meant what I said, but I wasn't sure if she'd believe me. Hell, I wasn't sure I believed me.

"I trust you, Tom. And I never trusted that little runt the whole time he was talking to me. The agent wanted to see the rental records for the week before the Fourth of July, but he didn't ask me about anyone specifically by name."

"Never said the name Andy Hood?"

"Never. It was almost like he was just going through the motions of checking our records but hardly looked at them when I gave them to him."

"Are these records public? I mean, would he normally need a court order to check them?"

"Not really. We do things informally here on the coast. You know that if you lived here even a few years."

I nodded. "Yeah, I know what you mean. So, he glanced at the records and then left? That's really peculiar."

"I guess it is, but I just thought he was checking my records and hotels in case somebody stood out—I mean for his investigation. I had forgotten the whole thing until you asked me about it."

"You never heard from him again?"

"Never, thank goodness. I wouldn't like to meet him in a dark alley. I didn't like that little runt. Kind of a mean nerd, if you ask me. And he talked funny too."

I laughed. "My sentiments exactly."

I was astounded that Agent Rutland had done such a careless investigation. To me, that indicated that he was not interested in finding any other suspects for the bombing once he had snared Michaela.

"Okay then, I have a question for you: do you remember a man who gave his name as Andy Hood?"

She shook her head. "I get lots of people in here, and I forget their names."

"I understand perfectly. Another question: can I see the records for that week?"

"You bet. I want to help your friend." She got up, opened a file drawer, and pulled out a folder, which she placed on the desk in front of me.

"Be my guest. I need to go to the little girls' room."

The folder was labeled *July 1 to 15* and contained copies of rental agreements. I leafed through the pages and soon found what I was looking for. On July 3, a Ford Thunderbird had been rented for a week to someone named *Andrew Hood*. According to Agnes's notes attached to the agreement, the man had returned it after business hours on July 4 with a less than full gas tank. For all car rental companies, this was one of the biggest sins a customer can commit, short of wrecking the car. Agnes had attempted to track Hood down to collect the extra charge because the credit card he had used was no longer accepted. Her notes said that his phone had been disconnected.

Hood had used a 503 phone number. I dialed it immediately.

"The number you have dialed is no longer in service. The number has been changed."

Odd that Hood's new number was so freely given. I dialed the new number, which had a Lincoln City area code.

"Drift Creek Car Customizing Service is not open today," said the recording. "Please leave your name and number, and we will return your call to set up an appointment."

I hung up as Agnes walked back into the room.

"I see from your notes that you tried to track our friend down. You ever think about becoming a detective?"

"Honey, when you've been in this business as long as I have, you need to be a detective and a marriage counselor and get involved in a lot of things I don't care to mention." Then Agnes laughed very loudly.

"Ever hear of Drift Creek Car Customizing Service?" I asked her.

"Can't say that I have." She pulled out a directory from a rack on her desk. "Here they are. Looks like they're up Drift Creek Road a ways, probably on the way to the falls. Funny place for a business, but we've got all kinds of weird things going on in the mountains. I'll bet it's a front for something or other you probably shouldn't get involved in."

"People have been telling me that all my life."

I stood up and held out my hand.

"Agnes, I can't thank you enough. What you've told me and showed me helped a lot and will probably help my friend to dodge a real nasty situation. I will never use your name, and I wasn't here."

Agnes grabbed my hand so forcefully that one of her dangling bracelets came loose and fell onto the desk with a clank.

"Honey, it has been my pleasure." And then she winked one of her blue-tinted eyelids.

DRIFT CREEK ROAD INTERSECTS HIGHWAY 101 about a half-mile south of the Lincoln City area known as Cutler City. I knew the area well because some old friends of mine had once been directors of a church summer camp in the Coast Range. This road was the one I took when I visited them. I knew that in a few miles it changed from a flat, well-maintained highway to little more than a gravel-topped and curvy trail that was dangerous and impassible in the winter.

I also knew that Andy Hood had picked this area as a place to hide for a reason. The Coast Range's spectacular canyons and creeks and forests concealed a multitude of dangers. Marijuana flourished in the wet climate. The people who grew, harvested, and sold it for big money did not like outsiders intruding on their carefully concealed plantations, and that applied to state police officers and sheriff's deputies, as well as to me on my current quest.

As I turned onto Drift Creek Road, I could not be sure how far in the business was located. I doubted it even existed and figured that Hood had used it when renting the car because he had to look as harmless as possible. I pulled over as soon as I could and called Lorenzo. Foolhardy as I was, I realized I needed to tell someone where I was going. I consoled myself with the fact that I had done many foolish things in my life. This couldn't be worse than some of those.

"Is Lorenzo in? This is Tom Martindale. I'm one of his clients."

Static filled the air as I strained to hear his secretary's reply.

"Could you repeat that please? I'm having trouble hearing you."

More static, but this time I made out her answer.

"Oh. Not until later today. Tell him I called and be sure to give him my cell phone number."

I gave it to her.

"And *señorita*? Tell him I am going up into the Coast Range on Drift Creek Road. Drift Creek. Yes. He knows where it is or can find it. *Gracias*."

I turned off the phone and put it in the console next to me. No one could reach me up here because I doubted there were cell towers this far into the wilderness. I was probably on my own in more ways than one. I got back onto the road and headed east.

The trees on the hill ahead of me had been mowed down by a clear-cut. The timber companies that own the forests around Oregon not managed by the state and federal governments care little about public opinion when they decide to cut their trees. Although they eventually replant the ravaged hillsides that are left behind, the regrowth process takes many years.

As I continued my drive, I passed tidy stick-built homes and both neat and rundown mobile homes and trailers. Here and there old farmhouses dotted the landscape. More often than not, the yards were littered with old car bodies and rusted farm equipment. Someone once told me that some rural people make their places as despoiled and unattractive as possible to outwit the tax assessor. I'm not sure of that, but I do know that these derelict buildings are certainly an open sore on the pristine landscape around them. In a few more miles, the smooth pavement changed to gravel and my car began generating clouds of dust. The road climbed gradually, and the terrain changed from flat fields to rather dense forests of Douglas fir and hemlock.

In a few more miles, I came to my destination. Although there was no address in sight, I saw a battered sign lying in a ditch. Only the words *Creek* and *Cust* were visible. The narrow road into the property was barred by a heavy steel cable. I drove on and soon spotted an area shaded by trees and not all that visible from the road. I stopped my car in a cloud of dust and got out.

I walked down the road and passed the blocked entrance. Before long, I came to a clearing that contained the ruins of an old building. It looked like it hadn't been used for anything in years, let alone customizing cars. I circled around it and peered into the dirty windows. The building was empty. In front of the only door, a slip of paper caught my eye. I smoothed it out. It was a parking permit for Drift Creek Falls.

*   *   *   *   *

As I drove into the trailhead parking lot a half-hour later, I recalled reading a description of the unique suspension bridge over the falls. The copywriter had called it "a cross between the Golden Gate Bridge and one of the bridges than span the Himalayan gorges." Even Forest Service public affairs people can get carried away at times.

No other cars were parked in the lot—unusual for this time of year. I paid the $5 day fee and walked onto the trail. It had been expertly cleared, and I made good time. The bridge was imposing. Despite its steady sway, the structure was sturdy. I walked across it slowly, pausing in the middle to look down about a hundred feet to Drift Creek. When I got to the other side, I glanced back at the falls—I'd guess about a 75-foot torrent of water fell into a pool below before rushing into the creek itself.

I looked up at the forest canopy above me. It was a combination of both second-growth trees and a few old-growth trees. The stillness would have been soothing had I not been so on edge. Although I doubted that anyone was watching me in this beautiful place, paranoia did not seem misplaced.

From the place where visitors usually stopped to admire the view and take photos, I spotted an opening farther down the creek bank and walked to it. There a path headed deeper into the forest. Walking was harder here because the brush had not been cut. Ruts from winter rains made walking difficult. After a few miles, I spotted a high chain-link fence topped with barbed wire. Just the thing to keep custom cars from escaping after they had been detailed.

I kept out of sight in the trees as I walked along to see if I could find any buildings. Before long, I saw smoke rising from a two-story log house that looked fairly new. In contrast to some of the houses I had seen on my drive up here, this house and the yard immediately around it were neat and well maintained. Next to the house stood a one-story building that looked like a bunkhouse. To the side of both was a large area that had been cleared of all vegetation and seemed to be some kind of assembly point. A small stage stood at one end. It had a podium with stanchions to hold flags to the left and right of the center.

The more I saw, the more I came to realize that this was a training camp. For some kind of underground group? Right-wing militia? Religious cult? I moved away from the fence so I could keep hidden in the trees while I thought this over.

I pulled out the binoculars I had put in my pocket when I left my car and scanned the scene in front of me. Before long, a door in the bunkhouse opened and a man in a long, white robe walked out carrying a flag. He walked onto the stage and inserted the flag into one of the stanchions. He unfurled it and smoothed the wrinkled surface.

It was also white and had a blue and yellow circle in the center. I focused the binoculars on the emblem and could make out some kind of Arabic writing. Just then, I heard a loud crash in the brush behind me. I closed my eyes and braced for a blow to my head, either by hand or by bullet.

AFTER A FEW SECONDS OF STANDING AS STILL AS I COULD,
I dared to turn my head and look toward the sound. If someone was
about to shoot me, I wanted them to have to look me in the eyes
when they pulled the trigger. At first, I saw nothing in the clearing
behind the grove of trees where I was hiding. A second later, one of
the largest elk I had ever seen looked up from his afternoon meal of
salmonberries and grass but barely took note of me.

A few years ago, I had written a report for an environmen-
tal group about wildlife in the state. In doing research for that
freelance job, I recalled that the Roosevelt elk that inhabit the
mountains of western Oregon and Washington can stand as tall
as five feet and weigh as much as a thousand pounds for males
and six hundred pounds for females. I had even gone on a field
trip with several people in that organization to see some of the
species I was discussing. The elk I remember seeing were a lot
smaller than this big guy. As I watched, he was soon joined by
several females, who also began eating.

I backed up slowly and turned to walk along the fence as unob-
trusively as possible. I wanted to see how far back the fence extended
and if there were any openings I could slip through.

After fifteen minutes, I came to a post that indicated a corner of the property. An equally high fence extended at a right angle across the back of the property. In a few minutes, I came upon several more large male elk that were taking turns charging the fence as if they wanted to knock it down. The sound of their antlers hitting the metal reverberated throughout the quiet forest. I quickly moved back to hide in the trees and watch.

Before long, several men carrying rifles ran up to the other side of the fence and began chattering in what was probably Arabic. They watched with terror in their eyes as these great beasts repeatedly slammed against the barrier, but the fence would probably protect them—at least for now. They conferred and after more chattering, one of the men stepped closer to the fence and fired his weapon into the air. The noise caused the elk to stop for a few seconds. Then they resumed their ramming.

Now all of the men lined up along the fence and fired their rifles into the air. They also shouted what sounded like "shoo, shoo." One removed his turban and waved the white cloth at the elk. That move was apparently enough for the largest animal; he turned and walked away slowly, with the others in his entourage following close behind.

The men nodded and patted one another on the back. The man who had waved his turban wound it around his head, and the group walked back into the forest, no doubt talking happily about their triumph. I decided to wait a while before checking the fence to see if the elk had weakened it, so I sat down on a stump.

After a half-hour, I stood up and made my way to a point in the fence where a large clump of brush was growing right up to it. This would allow me some cover while I checked for any weak links. The structure held firm in both directions. I was about to give up when I noticed an area where the links in the wire had broken and parted slightly. Even this heavy steel was no match for the powerful head of a bull elk—or two or three of them.

The shadows of the long summer afternoon were beginning to fall on the area where I now dared to stand. I yanked on the loose metal and was able to pry it out, at first only slightly, then larger and larger so that in five minutes, I had created a hole big enough for me to step through. Unfortunately, one of my fingers was bleeding by this time and the blood was dripping onto my pants. I pulled my handkerchief out of a pocket and tied it as tightly as I could around the wound.

As soon as I was safely inside the fence, I ran to my left to hide in the trees while I figured out what to do next. Although I would be no match for men with rifles, I hoped I could hang around long enough to see if the illusive Andy Hood was in this compound. If I could prove to the authorities that he existed, Michaela might be released.

I ran from tree to tree to a point where the buildings I had seen from the other side were below me, down a slight decline in the ground. As I neared what I thought of as a bunkhouse, I saw the men who had been at the fence and five others lined up in two rows doing exercises on the other side of the building. What differed from the calisthenics I had done in P.E. classes in school was that the men were using their rifles in the drill.

I crept away from where they were and headed toward the two-story house closer to the entrance. No one appeared to be inside so I chanced a peek in the sliding glass door that led in from the deck. At first, the room seemed to be empty. Then I noticed some movement on a couch that faced a fireplace. I leaned forward for a better view and could clearly see a tall, good-looking man and an equally attractive woman making passionate love. He fitted the description of the man who had rented the car: dark-skinned and Middle Eastern. This had to be Andy Hood.

I walked back into the woods to watch things for a while. In a few minutes, the man who had been leading the others in the exercises walked up on the deck and flung open the door. He seemed surprised to see the woman and immediately started shouting in Arabic. From my vantage point in the trees, I could see him pull Hood away from the woman and then yank her to her feet. She screamed as he threw some clothes at her and turned his back while she dressed. Hood shouted at the man, who seemed to be paying no attention to him.

As soon as the woman had finished dressing, the man grabbed her by the arm and led her out of my sight. I heard her crying and then a door slammed. After that, the sound of her voice was faint, as if she had been locked in a closet. By this time, Hood had put clothes on and was again arguing loudly with the man. He pulled Hood out the door and pushed him toward the exercise area.

This might be my chance to go inside to see if I could find anything we could use to identify Hood or whatever his name really was. I opened the door and stepped inside. The place was a mess, with half-eaten food on paper plates and cans of soft drinks on every surface. The air reeked of grease and cigarette smoke.

After each step, I paused to listen for sounds—nothing but the distant shouts of the men doing their exercises. The woman in the closet next to the front door was silent. When I walked by the door, however, she heard me.

"Is someone there? Andy, is it you? Get me out of this fuckin' hole. I don't deserve this."

I ignored her and walked cautiously up the stairs. There were four bedrooms on the second floor and a bathroom at the end of the hall. It really smelled up there—of sweat and uneaten food and the aftermath of sex. In the second room on the left, I spied a photo tacked to the wall with pushpins, which I took down to examine more closely. In it, Hood was dressed in a long, white robe and long headdress held in place by a gold-colored cord. A long dagger hung from another cord around his waist. He had his arm around a pretty blond woman, who was looking up at him. I looked around the room for something to take with me in addition to the photo.

I soon found what I was looking for—a letter signed by "Abdul Hakim" and a glass, which I wrapped in a sock I found on the floor. I hoped it would have his fingerprints on it. For good measure, I grabbed a toothbrush from the dresser for more of Hood's DNA.

Then I heard the sliding door open below. I stopped for fear any step would cause a creak in the wooden floorboards that could be heard below.

"Is someone there? Andy, is that you?" It was the woman in the closet.

I waited.

"ANDY? GET ME THE FUCK OUTTA HERE!"

Then she started to scream loudly. I used the noise to step to the window. I opened it carefully and stepped out onto the roof. Luckily for me, it was built at a gradual angle. I let myself slide to the edge where I could step onto the roof of the lower part of the house. It was at the rear so it was probably a laundry room. As I did that, I heard more voices from the other men going into the main room.

"HELP ME! GET ME OUTTA THIS STINKIN' HOLE, YOU DIRTY RAG HEADS!"

As I hit the ground, I heard the door of the closet open and a loud bang as it hit the wall next to it. Then, as I ran back into the woods, I heard more shouting from the men and a chilling sound: a single shot rang out.

I SPENT MOST OF THE DRIVE BACK TO NEWPORT looking in my rearview mirror. I was amazed to have gotten in and out of the compound without anyone seeing me. Oddly, I hadn't thought about what I would do or say had I been discovered. I was used to relying on luck and my ability to talk my way out of tight spots. This tactic had worked in my journalism career and helped me get people to tell me things they probably should not have told me. In the academic world, the ability to fabricate and camouflage was sometimes just as necessary, but the people were less gullible.

It was in my third career as an author that luck had played the most pronounced part in my success. First, I had become involved in a number of situations where I had put myself in danger in an effort to help friends. I hated to admit to anyone—let alone myself—that this work made me an amateur detective. Luck played a role several times because I was not killed or arrested. That I solved several crimes only served to feed my ego and impel me to repeat the process time and again.

Here is where more luck came in. I had written about what I did in helping capture the cocaine gang and now had published a book that was already selling well. I might write about the bridge bombing and the misuse of the Patriot Act in another book. None of this would have happened had I remained isolated in the halls of academe.

As soon as I reached my house, I used a cell phone to call both Lorenzo and Paul Bickford. I told them I needed their help but said they would have to trust me because I did not want to talk over the phone.

Both agreed without argument to meet me at the Portland International Airport the next morning. Lorenzo was already in town for Michaela's next hearing. Bickford said he would fly from wherever he was on the first available military plane he could find.

After hanging up, I went inside and fixed some eggs, toast, and coffee after I realized I hadn't eaten since morning. I was taking the last bite when someone knocked at the door. I opened it to find someone I hoped I would not have to see again.

"Agent Rutland. What brings you out on this fine summer night?"

"Evening, Martindale. May I come in?"

"I've been away and I'm kinda tired. Can it wait?"

Rutland snapped his fingers and four men quickly joined him on my front walk. He handed me a folded sheet of paper.

"This is a warrant to search your house. Please stand aside or I will have to ask one of these fine gentlemen with me to move you aside."

I complied with his request and even moved my arm in a wide and exaggerated swath like a ringmaster signaling the start of the circus. I kept smiling as the men walked around me. I wasn't sure why Rutland had convinced a judge that he needed to search my house again. He had not found anything the first time. I had barely been here in the weeks since.

I had nothing to hide then and nothing to hide now, with one exception, a big one—the letter with Hood's signature, the photo, and the glass covered with his fingerprints.

"It's kind of stuffy in here, Agent Rutland," I said, after a few minutes of watching the men invade my privacy. "Mind if I step outside until you finish?" I grabbed my coat from the back of a chair and put it on.

"No, Martindale. Go ahead and clear your head. This won't take too long."

I walked out the front door and then circled around to the back where I paused to look out to sea. I stood there for ten minutes before I heard the back door open.

"We're done here, Martindale," said Rutland.

I turned to face him.

"Find anything you're taking away that I should know about? What were you looking for anyway? Maybe I can help you find it."

Rutland was walking toward me. "You know I'm not at liberty to reveal that," he smiled.

"Why do you people always say that—'not at liberty'? What does that mean, really?"

"It means that I know something you don't know but would like to know. You know, Martindale, your way of speaking to the authorities will get you into trouble someday."

"That's what the former sheriff used to tell me. He was always trying to arrest me for this crime or that."

"Did he ever succeed?"

"Naw. He never did. He got killed last year when I found out he was taking bribes from a nasty drug lord. I miss him. I guess you're taking his place as my chief harasser."

I had stepped, or was about to step, over the line with Rutland. I knew it, but I couldn't seem to stop myself. Instead of getting huffy and threatening, however, Rutland just smiled.

"Until next time."

As he turned to walk away, I put my hands into the pockets of my jacket. For all the world knew, I was getting a bit chilly in the evening air and putting my hands in my pockets to warm them. But what I was really doing was making sure that Hood's letter and photo were still in one pocket and the glass containing his fingerprints in the other.

JULY 14, 2007

I WAS WIDE AWAKE AND A BIT JITTERY after my encounter with Rutland and his FBI teammates, so I decided to drive to Portland that night. I booked a room en route at a hotel near the airport, then called both men to suggest we meet there. After the two and a half-hour drive, I checked in and was asleep in seconds. I did not wake up until the alarm rang at 6 a.m.

I was eating breakfast in the coffee shop off the lobby when Lorenzo walked in. We embraced, and he sat down opposite me.

"How are you, Tom? You look beat. This full-time sleuthing is taking its toll on you."

I pulled down the skin below both eyes to make the bags even more prominent than they were. "I need some kind of face peal or youth serum," I groaned, "or I'm headed into Elephant Man territory."

I glanced at him, his perfect teeth shining out from his blemish-free brown face.

"You, on the other hand, look like Ricardo Montalbán at the height of his career."

"Who?"

"God, that makes me feel real old. He was a handsome Latin movie star of the 1940s, 1950s, and 1960s."

"Oh, yeah. He did Chrysler commercials and played on that TV show *Fantasy Island* with that midget."

"Whatever. You remember him your way, I'll remember him mine. You never look tired or old. That's what I meant."

"I sure feel tired and old, especially after working on Michaela's case. I'm being stopped at every turn by this damned Patriot Act. I never realized how zealous the government could be in cases that are brought under it. Even if they make a mistake in detaining someone—like with Michaela—they are reluctant to admit it. They seem to try extra hard to keep that person locked up. I can't get them to budge in her case. Not without some new evidence. They've got her fingerprint and that is that."

I glanced around the room before talking.

"As soon as Paul gets here, we'll go up to my room and I'll tell you what I've found out. I think we need to be careful about what we say in public. The walls could have ears."

As if on cue, Bickford walked in the main door and began to scan the crowd in the lobby. I got up and motioned for him to join us.

"I'm not sure if you two have met. Paul Bickford, this is my friend and attorney, Lorenzo Madrid. Lorenzo, this is Major Paul Bickford, United States Army. He is also a good friend of mine, much to his regret."

Paul and Lorenzo ordered big breakfasts, and we engaged in a lot of small talk while they ate. After a half-hour, we got up and rode the elevator to my room.

The room was actually two rooms, with a bedroom in the rear and a living room with a sofa, some chairs, and a desk near the hall door.

"How did you rate this?" said Bickford as he walked around, no doubt looking for listening devices or assassins in the closet.

"I checked in late, and it was all they had. I figured we could use the extra space. If you need to stay over, Paul, you can bunk here. This sofa makes out into a bed."

"I might do just that," he said, sitting down.

Lorenzo and I sat in the chairs.

"I will dispense with the 'you're probably wondering why I called you all together' jokes and get to the point. I have found the illusive Andy Hood—or as you told me, Paul—Abdul Hakim. He is holed up in some kind of Islamic training camp in the Coast Range south of Lincoln City."

Both Lorenzo and Paul looked startled.

Bickford spoke first. "By *found* I assume that you followed him there and hung around and tried to engage him in some way."

"Not really *engage* him, if you mean talk to him," I answered proudly. "But I did get his fingerprints and a sample of his handwriting."

"TOM," shouted Bickford, "YOU ARE AN IDIOT! Ever since I first met you in the Arctic you have put yourself in harm's way constantly. We already found out in New York that these guys mean business. Hell, that one guy tried to kill us both!"

"You didn't tell me about that," said Lorenzo.

"I was getting around to it," I said.

"Yeah, he'd tell you if he had to, but maybe you'd be hearing it from me as we sat around looking at his dead body. I've talked to him until I'm blue in the face, but he won't listen to anyone. We have this mutual friend, Maxine March, and she told me . . ."

Bickford stopped in mid-sentence, I suppose deciding that even the mention of Maxine's name brought back bad memories for me.

I ignored the reference. "Do you want to beat up on me or hear what I have to say?"

Bickford shook his head. "Yeah, yeah. Go on. I'll cringe later."

I told them about tracking down Hood through the rental car information and going to the compound in the woods near the falls and getting in through the hole in the fence made by the elk and sneaking into the building and going into Hood's room and the woman who was thrown into the closet.

When I was finished, Lorenzo spoke first.

"You know you could have been killed, Tom. These guys are fanatical enough to shoot you on sight. Your foolishness aside, this does give me some leverage if I can prove that this Hood or Hakim or whoever he is fired at the bridge and that there was no connection between him and Michaela. The government has never said she fired the gun. She was, of course, playing in the orchestra in front of a hundred people at the time. What they *have* done is drag her into this as part of a terrorist conspiracy. If we can find out how he managed to plant her fingerprint on the shell casing, I can get her cleared and released."

"That's a big 'if', Lorenzo," said Bickford. "If our good friend here spooked them by his presence at the camp, they've probably long since cleared out."

"They didn't see me," I said. "I got in and out free and clear. The woman in the closet heard me, but she was shot before she could say anything."

"Oh, what bad luck for her," said Bickford, shaking his head. "I won't even go there now. It boggles my mind that this camp has been set up so close to civilization. I mean, a lot of people must visit that bridge every month. What are the authorities around here doing besides sitting on their asses and drinking coffee?"

"If they're all like our friend Agent Rutland, they get fixated on one suspect—in this case, Michaela—and quit looking for anyone else," I said.

"Yeah, he does seem to have a one-track mind," said Bickford. "And he would also love to get you behind bars. What is it with you and law enforcement types? That sheriff hated you for years. What do you do to these guys?"

"They can't match my superior intelligence," I said with a somber face, before breaking out into laughter.

"I think they think you interfere too much and forget your place," added Lorenzo. "You are too pushy."

"It's the reporter in me, I guess. I don't take no for an answer. And I also try to help my friends."

"Save the sanctimony, Tom," said Bickford. "Some of that may be true, but you know you love the danger. And now that you're running with the big dog authors, you can write about all of this stuff and get rich. In the meantime, all of us peons below you in the pecking order have to scramble to clean up your messes."

I didn't protest because Bickford was right. I was guilty of everything he accused me of.

"So, what do we do now?" I asked.

Lorenzo turned to Bickford.

"If I could find out more about this Hood/Hakim guy, I could plot a strategy that shifted the blame for the bridge incident to him and away from my client, Michaela Ross. That would be a start, at least. Then I would need to figure out how her fingerprint got on the shell casing."

"I've got some friends at the local Alcohol, Tobacco, and Firearms office here, and they'll run his print for me," said Bickford. "Where is it?"

I walked over to my jacket and pulled out the glass I had carefully wrapped up at the compound. I pulled out the photo and the letter too.

"I hope I didn't smudge it," I said, as I handed it to Bickford.

He lifted it up to the ceiling light. "It looks pretty clear. Not bad for an amateur. You get that out of your Nancy Drew Sleuthing Guidebook?"

"I prefer the Hardy Boys version."

We all laughed.

"I picked up these too." I gave him the letter. "This has his handwriting on it and also gives us his real name."

"How do you know this came from his room?" asked Bickford.

"This photo of him in Arab dress was hanging on the wall."

Bickford nodded and looked at the photo.

"Who's the woman?"

He handed the photo back to me.

"To tell you the truth, I didn't really look at it."

"I've also got to figure out what to do with this whole crew up there," continued Bickford. "We can't have any would-be terrorists running around in the Oregon forests. But I have no jurisdiction to even look into this. And I have no evidence that these men are not a religious community communing with nature."

I shook my head and jumped to my feet. "I'm telling you, Paul, religious acolytes don't keep guns around, and they don't . . ."

Bickford held up his hand. "You may be right, but I've got to have proof before I send the ATF and the Oregon State Police in there with guns blazing."

He looked at the piece of paper I had given him.

"Have you looked at this, Tom?"

"Not really, only Hakim's signature."

"It's a request to the Saudi embassy in Washington for funds. You recall the former ambassador's wife was involved in an Islamic charity that was accused of providing funding to al-Qaeda. This gives us the link we need to go forward. Boy, are the faces of your pal Agent Rutland and the local law enforcement types going to be red over this one. A whole gang of terrorists is training right under their noses. How could they miss them?"

"I'll tell you how. They were busy taking the easy way out by throwing Michaela in jail," I said.

"Yeah, yeah, yeah," said Bickford. "You keep saying that, and I believe you, but we need proof. This letter and the fingerprints on this glass may give it to us. Tell you what . . . let me make some calls and get this print analyzed. Then you and I are going to take a ride, Tom. Much as I hate to admit it, I need your help to lead me to this training camp. God knows why I would bring you of all people along, but I have no other choice. You got your bulletproof cap and gown in that closet over there?"

As he was talking, I looked again at the photo of Hood. "I knew this woman looked familiar, but I couldn't place her."

I handed the photo to Bickford, and Lorenzo got up to look at it over his shoulder.

"The blond is Sheila Cross, the cellist who was shot at the same time the artillery shell was hitting the bridge."

BICKFORD FOUND ME AN ARMY CAMOUFLAGE fatigue uniform, which I put on at the hotel, even though it was a size too big for me. I felt ridiculous but he insisted, saying that we needed to blend into the trees. He was dressed the same, although his ensemble was tailored to his trim physique and made him look like a model on an Army Special Ops recruiting poster.

He had spent a lot of time on the telephone before we checked out and left for the coast. He had a four-wheel-drive pickup delivered to the hotel. Now, he huddled in the parking lot with six men who looked like his kid brothers. All were wearing army camo and were slim and trim and tanned, with shaved heads. I had no idea where he'd gotten them and knew he wouldn't tell me if I asked. He talked to them in low tones just out of earshot.

For his part, Lorenzo had agreed to prepare a new motion for Michaela's release based on the new evidence—the letter to the Saudi charity. Bickford had already sent Hood/Hakim's fingerprints to yet another mysterious government operative. It would provide more proof that Lorenzo could use in court.

The question of Hood/Hakim's relationship with Sheila Cross was another issue entirely. Michaela had not been accused of involvement in her death. Indeed, no one had. It seemed that the FBI cared little about her, focused as they were on the terrorist incident at the bridge. I had not heard that the local police were even doing much investigation. I suspected that Hood/Hakim was involved in her killing but had no way to prove it now. Maybe we could solve two crimes by solving one.

While Bickford and I drove back to the coast, Lorenzo was going to press his old investigator, Ray Pearl, back into service to see what he could find out about Sheila Cross.

"Quit sneaking looks at all of those hot young guys, Lorenzo," I said with a smile on my face.

"I don't know what you're talking about," he smiled back. "Actually, I am so out of it now that all I can do is look."

"I doubt that," I said. "Look at all the heads you turn when we go out to eat. All those young waitresses—and waiters—go gaga over you."

We stopped talking as Bickford turned and walked over to us. The men he had been talking to got into a black SUV and sped away.

"So, what's the plan, Paul?" I asked.

"Better if you don't know the details. Let's just say I've got some things lined up for our friends at that compound."

He turned to Lorenzo.

"Thanks for helping with this. I'll keep you in the loop about the fingerprints and anything else you might use in court. When do you appear again?"

"Tomorrow at 10 a.m. Send me anything you get, and I'll add it to my new motion. You've got my cell number. I'm also using an office here in Portland that I rent for when cases are tried here. Here's the fax number."

"Okay, guys," I said. "It seems like momentous occasions like this need a valedictory. I really value both of your friendships and thank you for everything you've done for me over the years."

"Get in the car, Tom," said Bickford with a smirk. "I don't plan to get shot down there, and I don't plan to let you get injured either."

"I know, I know, but I wanted to let you know . . ."

"Say 'Goodbye, Lorenzo'."

"Goodbye, Lorenzo."

∗ ∗ ∗ ∗ ∗

Bickford is not much for small talk so we spent long stretches on the drive to the coast in total silence. I dozed and made passing comments now and then. He usually grunted and kept his eyes on the road.

"Go ahead and ask me about Maxine, if you want to," he said at one point.

I opened my eyes and yawned. "Is this some kind of truth-telling ritual, like around a campfire on a scary night?"

"Great. I start to open up, and you go all sarcastic on me. Fine," he said grimly.

"I just don't want to talk about her," I replied. "Our relationship has been over for about a year. I didn't want to face that before but seeing her in New York and seeing the two of you together crystallized things pretty well for me. I have moved on. I am getting too old to pursue someone if they don't want to be pursued. Most of what happened is my fault, and I accept that. It's easier if I do. Plus, she lives a whole continent away. And also, if you two are happy together, that's fine too. You are a good friend, and I guess our friendship means as much to me as staying involved with her."

Bickford drove a mile or so in silence.

"Truth be told, Tom, she and I had some good sex and some good dinners, but there's no future for us," he said. "You know the kind of life I lead. I'm never in the same place more than a few days. Hell, did you know I don't even have an apartment anymore? I have a few things in storage in D.C. and that's it. I'm a nomad, and I like it that way. A wife or even a steady girlfriend would just tie me down, hold me back. I need to be able to go into situations like this one without thinking about a loved one at home worrying about me. For me, there is no 'back home' anymore. And I like it that way."

"I'm not sure I believe you about Maxine, but thanks for letting me down easy."

He turned into a highway wayside and stopped. He turned to me and took hold of my arm.

"I'm not bullshitting you, Tom. I'm dead serious."

"Okay, okay. I believe you."

We reached the turnoff of Highway 101 and Drift Creek Road at 4:30 p.m. As often happened on the central Oregon coast this time of year, it was foggy and cloudy. As we climbed into the foothills of the Coast Range, shafts of sunlight penetrated the fog, then were obscured by it.

When we arrived at the parking lot for the falls, his men in the black SUV were already there. Bickford stopped our car some distance from them.

"Stay here," he said, as he got out of the car and walked over to them. No other cars were in the lot. The men gathered around him in a semicircle and listened intently.

At one point, he pulled out a map and spread it over the hood of their vehicle. After a few minutes, he stopped talking and the group snapped to attention and saluted him. He returned their salute in an equally precise manner and then walked back to the car where I waited. One of the men followed him.

"Get out, Tom. Time to rock and roll."

I stepped out and smiled at the other man, who was young enough to be one of my students.

"Hello, I'm Tom Mar . . ."

"No time for niceties," Bickford said from the rear of the car where he was pulling a backpack from the trunk. "Let's get going."

I dropped my arm and followed Bickford up the trail. The young guy got into the car and drove it out of the parking lot behind the SUV.

After a few hundred yards, Bickford stopped on the trail. He motioned to me with a finger across his lips and listened. I heard only the chirping of birds and the faint sound of a plane high in the sky. He pointed to a barely distinguishable path on the right, and I followed him onto it. We walked through thick brush for a few minutes. Ahead, I could hear the roar of the falls.

Soon we reached an area above the falls, a perch from where we could see the bridge below. A man with a machine gun was standing at the opposite end, smoking a cigarette.

Bickford motioned for me to follow him away from the falls. There was no path here, and the thick brush made it difficult to walk. Periodically, Bickford would turn around and put a finger to his lips. I doubted anyone could hear us, however, because of the thunderous sound of the water cascading over the falls.

At some point, Bickford pointed to an area where the brush was less dense. We walked up to it, and I saw to my chagrin that we were at the top of a cliff with the creek directly below us.

"He can't see us here," Bickford whispered. "We're around the bend."

He pulled a long coil of rope from his backpack and tied one end to a tree. Then he let the rope unfold over the side of the cliff.

"I'm going to take you down there on my shoulders," he said. "All you have to do is drop down onto me once I'm in position—like they do when they pull people up into helicopters. You just hang onto the rope, and I'll back you up so you don't fall. Got it?"

"Paul, I weigh 185. You can't hold me up without falling down yourself. I can make it myself."

"Negative. For once in your life, pay attention to someone who knows more than you do. I don't have time to argue. Do what I say, or I will leave you here. I mean it!"

"Okay! Okay!"

The plan, which probably came out of a Special Ops training manual, worked well. Bickford went first and then I slid easily onto his shoulders, and he hoisted us both down. At the bottom, on the wet sand of the creek bed, Bickford backed up to a tree stump and I got off.

"Very smooth, Paul. Thanks."

At this point, the water of the creek was running fast but did not seem too deep. Paul stepped easily across on a partially submerged log. I tried to follow but when I got in the middle, the log shifted. I lost my footing and fell in. I grabbed hold of another log, but it broke free of the bank and headed toward the bridge. The quick movement of the log attracted the attention of the man high above, and he started firing his gun as soon as he saw my head sticking up. I looked around, but Bickford had disappeared.

The man fired several more bursts, so I held my breath and ducked underwater. I expected more bullets to whiz by me, but when I came up for air, all was silent. I propelled the log toward the shore and turned in time to see the man clutching his throat as Bickford tightened a wire around his neck. The man fell to the ground and Bickford ran to me.

"Are you hit?"

"No, I'm fine. Just a bit waterlogged."

He pulled me to my feet, and we both moved quickly onto the main trail. We walked for several miles and came to the same place in the fence I had slipped through. This time the hole was much larger, as if the elk were determined to reopen an old route. We stepped through.

At that moment, we saw the Arabs lining up in the same formation I had witnessed before. They were facing away from us toward a man who was shouting at them in Arabic—Hood/Hakim.

Like before, they were doing their calisthenics with their rifles. Each time they did knee bends or raised their weapons in the air, they shouted *"Allah Akbar."*

Bickford pulled out a small radio and said something I could not understand. Then he pulled out what looked like a whistle and blew it.

The mournful sound of an elk emerged. The men were so engrossed in their rituals that they ignored the new noise. Maybe elk sounds had become so common out here that they had gotten used to them.

Then I heard the loud thud of many hooves behind us as ten of the huge creatures ran toward the fence, herded along by Bickford's men. The elk slowed their momentum as they paused to go through the opening. Bickford started blowing his whistle again, and the animals picked up steam and ran right at the Arabs.

Hood/Hakim saw them first and reacted quickly. He started running for the house, but Paul stepped from our hiding place and shot him in the arm. He fell to his knees.

The others started shooting wildly at us and the elk. The large creatures thundered on and soon engulfed the hapless men before they could aim again. The elk circled and then slowly began to close in a kind of maze that left the men no way out.

Bickford and his men surrounded the strange mammalian assemblage and moved in carefully so as not to scare the big beasts. They soon had all of the men in plastic handcuffs. In patting down their robes, they found a number of guns and knives. Bickford's men made them get down on their knees to the side of the open space. One of Bickford's commandos threw a rope over an elk and led it toward the front gate. The other animals followed docilely.

"This was their traditional route to water," said Bickford. "This camp interrupted that. Now we'll reopen it for them by tearing down the fence."

"I guess you must have an elk specialist on call who figured that out," I said, shaking my head.

Soon, I heard the whirring engines of a helicopter, first in the distance, then right above us. A small chopper landed in the open space the elk had just exited.

"I'm going to get our friend here to Portland," Bickford shouted to me over the whine of the engines, which the pilot had not shut off. "They're sending a bus for the others. You okay with riding back with one of my guys here?"

"Yeah, sure. We'll catch up tomorrow. He can take me to my car."

"Done," he said.

Bickford signaled for Hood/Hakim to be brought to the helicopter. By this time his arm had been bandaged by the medic who was part of the group. Although stumbling and moaning, he got to the aircraft fairly easily.

"You'll live," said Bickford, as he pushed him inside and then took a seat next to him. "Remember, I shot you in your arm, not your leg!"

As the pilot took off, Bickford looked down and gave me a thumbs-up. I thought I saw a smile on his face, but with Bickford, you can never be sure of anything.

JULY 15, 2007

NEITHER MY RECURRING NIGHTMARE about the lighthouse nor memories of the events of the past few weeks kept me awake that night. I slept twelve hours, a rarity for me in recent years. I might have been out for several more if the telephone had not rung.

I fumbled for the phone and answered hoarsely.

"Hello."

"Tom, you sound odd. It's Lorenzo. Are you okay?"

"Yeah. I haven't used my voice in so long it sounds funny. How are things going?"

"That's why I called. I need to see you as soon as possible."

"Sure. Give me a chance to shower and eat something and then drive to Portland. Maybe three hours from now."

"No, Tom. That won't be necessary. I'm in Newport. Shall we say one hour?"

"Newport?"

My mind was hazy as if I had a bad hangover, but I hadn't drunk a drop of anything stronger than coffee for days.

"Sure, okay. Do you know where I live?"

"I don't want to come there. Meet me at the Performing Arts Center. You know where it is?"

"Yeah. But why there? It'll be closed, and I'm not sure how to get in. If you need to reconstruct the night of the concert and the shooting, you know the orchestra was playing outdoors—at the Coast Guard station near the bridge."

It was not like Lorenzo to get his facts so wrong. What was this all about?

"Just meet me there at 10:30—an hour and a half from now."

"Okay. I'll be there, but I wish you'd tell me what this is all about."

Lorenzo hung up without saying anything more.

I quickly showered and ate some cereal, not bothering to turn on the television news or even glance at the morning newspaper.

* * * * *

I pulled into the parking lot of the Performing Arts Center in a little over an hour. I was surprised to see the lot half full of cars. Either there was some kind of morning meeting or a rehearsal was going on inside.

As I walked to the front door, I saw Matt, the tall bass player from the orchestra, going in the door musicians use to get inside. Obviously, a rehearsal was going on for some special summer concert. I had been out of town so much the past few weeks that I hadn't known about it. Actually, the memory of what happened on the Fourth of July was fresh enough in my mind that I wasn't sure I could attend another concert for a while.

The door to the outer lobby was unlocked, and I walked through it past the box office to the larger lobby and then opened one of the doors to the auditorium itself. I stepped inside and stood at the top of the aisle.

The full orchestra was tuning up, with Maestro Horatio Pine at the podium, unruly hair and all.

"Okay, people," he said to the players, many of whom seemed to be ignoring him. He tapped the podium with his baton. A few musicians looked up but just as many others ignored Pine. He tapped louder and began to raise his voice.

"Do you want to remain members of this orchestra or not?" He was shouting now. "I do have the ear of the board chairman, and I am taking names!"

That outburst got their attention.

"Good. I thought you would begin to see things my way."

He looked down at the pages of music in front of him and made a big production out of turning the pages, his hair bobbing up and down as he did.

"Mozart's *Symphony No. 39,* if you please, ladies and gentlemen."

He raised his baton and away they went, in perfect cadence and pitch, at least to my untrained ears. At some point in the piece, some members of the orchestra stopped playing. They were soon joined by others. Pine looked up with anger, until he saw that all of them were looking out at the auditorium. Soon, all of them were standing and applauding as a figure walked toward the stage from the aisle opposite the one where I was standing.

Michaela Ross hesitated at first, then walked briskly to the stage. Pine came to the side stairs and escorted her to the podium. There were tears in her eyes as she bowed to her colleagues.

By this time, Lorenzo was standing next to me, and we both cried and clapped along with everybody else.

"WHERE TO BEGIN," SAID LORENZO, a few hours later in my living room. He and Michaela had accepted my invitation for lunch, which I had thrown together with help from a local French café.

"Let me say first how much I owe the two of you," she said. She got up and walked over to us and hugged and kissed us several times.

"I would be learning how to play in the prison orchestra if it wasn't for you guys."

"Lorenzo did the heavy lifting," I said. "I just dug up some stuff for him to use."

"You're being modest, Tom, as usual," he said. "The 'stuff' you dug up was what caused the government to drop any pending charges against Michaela and release her."

"When did that happen?"

"Late yesterday. I asked for and got an afternoon hearing before the same judge who ordered her held. I presented the evidence against Hakim and the fingerprints sample, and that was all it took for the judge to act."

"And how did the FBI react to having their star suspect let out of jail?" I asked.

"Your pal Agent Rutland was there, and he did not look very

happy," said Lorenzo. "But the U.S. Attorney seemed to grasp the mistake that had been made and actually made the motion to let Michaela out."

"But what about the so-called incriminating fingerprint?" I asked. "I thought they had found one of hers on the shell casing."

"That is the strange part," he said. "It was actually Hakim's, but there were enough similarities to Michaela's to make the FBI detain her. Although the friction ridge patterns are thought to be unique in each one of us, there are occasional anomalies, like in this case. Against all odds, the prints of Hakim and Michaela were enough alike to lead the FBI to think they had their terrorist. Once Rutland saw that her middle name sounded Middle Eastern, he leapt to the conclusion that she was guilty. Even if he had found evidence leading to someone else, I doubt he would have explored it. In his mind, he had the guilty person. Period."

"Racial profiling of the worst kind," I said.

"Saying I am Middle Eastern because my mother felt a kinship with relatives in her past that she never met is really nuts," Michaela said.

"So Rutland quit looking, and we know what happened next," continued Lorenzo. "That is the danger of the Patriot Act. You are truly guilty until proven innocent, and that is hard to do when you are locked up. That is why I am working so hard to get that law overturned or at least modified. This case will help, and that's why I got involved."

"Lucky for me you did," said Michaela. "And lucky for me you decided to write a profile of me, Tom."

"So what's happened to Hakim?" I asked.

"He's in federal custody somewhere. Your friend Paul Bickford has arranged for a whole task force to look into his camp in the Coast Range and all the activities the group might have pulled off if you hadn't stumbled into their compound."

"Me and those elk," I laughed. "Unconventional members of my team but very effective nonetheless. What about Sheila Cross? Who killed her?"

"Another strange thing: a piece of metal from the bridge flew off when the artillery shell hit and landed in an artery in her neck. She died instantly."

"Hakim had nothing to do with it?"

"Nothing. It seems he liked to date blond American girls and has left a whole string of failed romances everywhere he lived, plus a few illegitimate kids. A few police reports said he liked his sex rough, but no one pressed charges. Sheila had a fling with him, but there was no connection to what happened to her or the bridge bombing."

"She always was one to sleep her way to where she wanted to go," said Michaela ruefully. "I have to feel sorry for her, even though I didn't like her very much."

"How did Hakim get assigned to fire that artillery piece?"

"He was not actually a member of the Oregon National Guard," said Lorenzo. "One of the members of his group was. The guy had lived in Newport for years and was actually as American as any of us. He was fairly light-skinned like Hakim and wore a mustache. Apparently, Hakim just showed up at the concert in uniform and no one paid much attention to the fact that he was the wrong guy. He knew about weapons from training he had gotten in the Middle East. When it was time, he had no trouble firing the cannon."

Lorenzo looked at his watch. "I've got to be getting back to Salem. A lot of new cases have piled up while I was working on this one. I'm on a team of attorneys trying to get the Patriot Act modified or repealed, so I've got work to do. Speaking of Bickford, he said he'd call you."

Michaela stood up and pulled us to her.

"Group hug time," she said. "I can never repay either of you."

After they left and I had cleaned up the dishes, I felt like going to my study and working on my new book for the first time in weeks. I had a few days before I would resume my book tour for *The Cocaine Trail*.

The words came easily as my fingers touched the keyboard of my computer:

> *Fingerprints, Roosevelt elk, and a faulty federal justice system were the last things in Michaela Ross's mind as she joined her fellow musicians on the Fourth of July to play the traditional holiday concert of the Oregon Coast Symphony Orchestra. Halfway through Tchaikovsky's 1812 Overture, Ross, a cellist, heard a loud boom and saw an artillery shell hit the Yaquina Bay Bridge above her. At the same time, the cellist to her right slumped in her chair.*
>
> *"I had heard that death could come in many different ways,"* she recalls, *"but never by cello."*

AS WE CLIMBED THE CIRCULAR IRON STAIRS *of the lighthouse, nudged along by the barrel of Maldanado's gun, I began to doubt that Maxine and I would come out of this alive. The horrific noise of the storm would mask the sound of gunfire or our screams. As always, the drug dealer had the upper hand. He had ruined both of our lives very easily.*

As we ascended, the beam of Maldanado's flashlight illuminated the walls of the tower, which were bright and shiny from a new coat of paint. The lighthouse restoration was almost complete after more than a year of work in often difficult weather conditions.

As we got to the lamp room at the top, just under the dome and light itself, the local sheriff, who was on the payroll of the drug dealer, pushed up through a door that was never opened to the public. It went out onto the wooden platform that had been built around the dome to allow workmen to replace the windows and paint and sandblast the rust-encrusted iron of the parapet and lantern housing. The lens had been covered to protect it from damage, and plastic sheathing had been draped over the top part of the lighthouse to shield the men from the incessant wind. We were standing in this temporary circular room that surrounded the dome.

Maldanado used a knife to cut a hole in the plastic sheathing that had been draped over the top part of the lighthouse to protect the workmen from the incessant wind. Through the hole we could see the upper part of the lighthouse and the surrounding area as no one had ever seen it before or ever would again. The view of the waves hitting the rocks with a force that sent spray this high—over one hundred feet up—took my breath away. Despite my fear, I gloried in what I was seeing.

Maldanado threatened us again and nodded to Sheriff Kutler, who moved toward us, his arms raised. Just then, Paul Bickford rushed out of the shadows under the iron girding of the lighthouse with such force that the sheriff went flying through the air and out the opening to the sea. Maldanado grabbed Maxine, but Bickford shot him in the neck and then pushed him out after the sheriff.

"You didn't see that," he said to the two of us. "Let's get out of here."

Maxine and I looked at each other and smiled, happy to be safe.

✳ ✳ ✳ ✳ ✳

I woke up with a start, but this time I wasn't sweating and my heart wasn't racing. I hoped I had experienced the last of those nightmares, but the way my life had been running lately, you just never know.